BODY AT THE CROSSROADS

A VIKING WITCH COZY MYSTERY

CATE MARTIN

Copyright © 2020 by Cate Martin

All rights reserved.

No part of this book may be reproduced in any form or by any electronic or mechanical means, including information storage and retrieval systems, without written permission from the author, except for the use of brief quotations in a book review.

Cover design by Shezaad Sudar.

Ratatoskr Press logo by Aidan Vincent.

ISBN 9781951439-32-3

❀ Created with Vellum

FREE EBOOK!

Like exclusive, free content?

If you'd like to receive "The Cat's Hammer," a free prequel short story to the Viking Witch Cozy Mystery series, plus a ton of other free goodies, go to CateMartin.com to subscribe to my monthly newsletter! This eBook is exclusively for newsletter subscribers and will never be sold in stores. Check it out!

CHAPTER 1

It was hard not to keep thinking of the phrase "for the last time," but those four words were haunting me as I moved from room to room through the only house I had ever known as home. I would check that nothing had been left in the closets or cupboards, that every surface was clean and free of dust. Then I would walk out of that room, and I would think my thoughts were only on the same tasks awaiting me in the next room, but then those four words would pop into my brain out of nowhere.

I was closing my bedroom door. For the last time.

I was opening the shower door to make sure the tile was still clean and bright, then leaving the bathroom my mother and I had shared since I was a toddler. For the last time.

I ended in the kitchen. The plan was to go out the back door and head to my little yellow Volkswagen that was stuffed with all of my personal belongings as well as my cat Mjolner, who had surely escaped from his crate by now. He always did.

But instead, I just came to a stop against the counter. I couldn't leave, not yet. But why? I was certain I hadn't forgotten anything. And yet I felt like I was waiting for something to happen. But there was nothing left to do at the house. The only task that remained was signing the final paperwork at the realtor's office in the morning.

I closed my eyes and tried to stop thinking entirely. Usually, when I was trying to remember something, this was the best way to summon it up. It's not that I have a bad memory; it's just that I tend to have a lot of things going on in my mind at any one time, and quieting everything down for a moment usually lets the less demanding thoughts rise to the surface.

I focused just on my breath at first, but then I heard the sound of birds outside the kitchen window, the brood that had hatched from the nest tucked into the drainpipe all mature now but still hanging close to home. Then a bus went by outside, the driver shifting expertly through the gears as he picked up speed.

I could smell the grass I had cut the day before, drying out in the sun that was technically early autumn but had the heat of late summer still. The clean smell of the grass mingled with the softer aroma of tea that always lingered in our kitchen.

I opened my eyes and looked around, but everything looked just the same. My thoughts weren't going to get any quieter than this. So what was I missing?

Then the phone on the wall rang, loud and jangling. The landline. I hadn't heard that phone ring in years; my mother had shut the ringer off when we both got our cellphones. When had it been turned back on?

It was surely a wrong number, but I picked it up anyway. I half-expected to hear the whine and beeps of a fax machine trying to send me something and didn't put the receiver against my ear right away. But when no sound came out of it at all, I pressed it to my ear. "Hello?" I said.

"Ingrid?" a woman asked. Her voice sounded familiar. Maybe one of my mother's friends, one who had missed the announcement in the paper for the wake but was calling now.

"This is she," I said.

"Ingrid, this is your grandmother, Nora Torfa."

I suppose in other, normal families that sentence might seem strangely formal. But I hadn't spoken to my grandmother in years. She hated telephones, my mother always told me, preferring letters and cards that I was, I admit, not the best at responding to.

The last call had been when I was ten, after my father had died. But that wasn't what I was remembering in that moment. No, what came back to me was the last time I had seen my grandmother face to face. That had been when I was eight, when my mother had started the long and ultimately futile search for a diagnosis for the disease that finally killed her. I had spent that entire summer at my grandmother's house, without my parents.

And until that very moment, I had forgotten it entirely. How was that possible?

But as a cascade of memories washed over me - images and sounds and tastes all in a jumble - I realized I hadn't forgotten entirely. I had just somehow thought I had dreamed it all. The vastness of Lake Superior shining like silver in the setting sun for as far as the eye could see. The strong smell of the fishings huts that dotted the shore where the fishermen gutted their catch, scraping the entrails into holes cut in the tabletops to fall into bins below. The taste of honey fresh from the comb, sticky and sweet.

But then other images started to mix in. These were things I had never forgotten; in fact, they always came back to me when I sat down to draw, but really had to have been from dreams. I suppose a summer spent in a fishing town populated by the descendants of Norwegian immigrants had had quite an influence on my young mind. I was forever after drawing pictures of the Norse gods, of trolls and crones, dwarves and elves. Vikings and their ships.

I had never actually seen such things, of course.

Had I? I felt so strange, like electric currents were dancing up and down my spine.

"Ingrid?" my grandmother said.

"Yes, sorry," I said. "I didn't expect to hear from you. I got your card."

"And the letter? Did you get my letter?" she asked.

"Oh," I said. But of course that was why she was calling. "I *did* get your letter."

"And?" she asked.

"I'm not sure this is a good time," I started to say, but it was like I couldn't hear my own words past the ringing of my ears. My skin felt all tingly, and my hair was rising on end. I looked around the kitchen as if I could see something causing all this, but what could I possibly expect to see? Some mad scientist in the doorway shooting me with a weird ray?

I realized that the feeling like I was waiting for something was gone now, but it had been replaced by another, more urgent feeling. Like I was about to make a decision, the most important decision in my life.

"This is precisely the right time," my grandmother said. "You have to come home now. Come to Runde."

Ah, I had forgotten that. Most Minnesotans pronounce the town "Roundie," like a nickname for a fat baby. But not my grandmother. She said it "Run-deh," with a u that sounded like if it were German, it would need an umlaut. She insisted that was how the original settlers had pronounced it, and I was never sure if she meant the settlers of the village founded in the 1880s on the north shore of Lake Superior, or if she meant their ancestors that had settled the island of the same name generations before back in Norway. Either way, she said it like she'd been there herself, at the founding and naming.

"I was planning to stay in the Twin Cities," I said. "I'm hoping to get a gig illustrating books, maybe sell a children's book of my own. I have some submissions out, but I haven't heard back yet."

"You can do that here as well as you can do there," she said gruffly. "Better, actually. It's cheaper to live here."

"But it's so remote," I said.

"We have the internet," she said, but she over-pronounced it, like it was a foreign word. "I know you're selling the house because you have to. Did you have somewhere there in town to stay? A friend with a spare room or something?"

"No," I admitted, glancing out the window at the car full of everything I had in the world. It all fit in a Volkswagen.

"Then you should come here," she said.

"I don't know," I said, but she cut me off.

"What are you feeling? Really feeling? Think before you answer."

I sucked in a breath as another memory hit me. That thing I do where I clear my mind to let the quieter thoughts come? She had taught me that when I was eight.

But I didn't need to do it again. I knew exactly what I was feeling. I had been picking up that letter several times a day since she sent it to me days before, and every time I did, the same two feelings struck me.

I really, really wanted to go. It was a deep feeling of longing so intense it almost scared me.

And I really, really didn't want to. And that feeling actually *did* scare me. Even now, with the memories coming back, I didn't know why I would be afraid to go back to a sleepy little town on the shore of Lake Superior, but I was. I was afraid.

"All right," my grandmother said as if I had said any part of that out loud. "Go to the window."

"How do you know I'm by a window?" I asked, looking around as if I was about to find a hidden camera somewhere.

"Why wouldn't you be by a window?" she asked and sounded annoyed. Well, she had called on the landline. It's not like people put those in dark basements or stuffy attics.

"Okay, I'm at the window," I said, leaning my belly against the edge of the gleaming sink.

"What do you see?" she asked.

"The juniper trees," I said. "The remains of a nest tucked between the drain pipe and the corner of the house. The maple in the back yard is starting to turn already. Too soon, tree."

My grandmother sighed. "Ingrid, focus. I'm asking you to look for a sign."

Had we had this conversation before?

"Mormor," I said, then hesitated. The word had just percolated up out of me, but not out of nowhere. I had called her that, when I was young. "Mormor," I said again, "I don't believe in signs or omens or any of that."

"No messages from the powers that be?" she asked leadingly.

"No, not really," I said and bit my lip.

"Well, good, because I told you before that was all nonsense," she said briskly. "Your mind is in conflict." I couldn't argue with that. "But you already know what you want to do; you just don't *know* you know it yet. Look around, and whatever jumps out at you is your answer."

"All right," I agreed.

At first, when I looked around, nothing seemed different. The colors on the maple were popping, but I wouldn't say they were jumping out at me. Or if they were, I had no idea what they were trying to tell me.

Then my eyes worked their way over to the yellow Volkswagen, the one with my whole life inside it. Then a black shape caught my eye.

Mjolner had gotten out of his travel crate. Really, he did this so often I don't know why I bothered ever putting him inside it. He was sitting calmly on the passenger seat, perched on top of a tall stack of my art portfolios, his tail carefully arranged around his over-sized paws. He was facing the front of the car, staring straight ahead through the windshield as if pretending to be driving somewhere.

Then he turned his head to look at me. The silver hammer pendant on his collar - the hammer that was his namesake - caught the light in a momentary flash.

Then he winked at me. Just a slow closing of his eye, an equally slow opening.

Sometimes something happens so fast you think you might have imagined it. This was just the opposite, so slow I wasn't sure it had even happened at all.

Then he resumed his previous position of staring straight ahead through the windshield.

"Ingrid?" my grandmother said.

"I'm coming," I said. "I have to go to the realtor's office to sign the papers in the morning, but after that, I'll drive up north. I should be there by midafternoon."

"Good," she said. "You still have the letter? Because you're going to need that map I drew for you."

"I have it," I said, although really all I would need was the address. The GPS on my phone would do the rest. But I had a feeling saying that to my grandmother was going to involve a lot of explaining. She didn't even like using landline phones; I could only imagine what she thought of smartphones.

"I'll see you then," my grandmother said, and then she hung up the phone.

I put the receiver back on the cradle then pulled my sleeve down over my hand to wipe my fingerprints off the hard plastic case.

My grandmother was right that I needed a place to stay, and that trying to stay in the city was going to be too expensive for a struggling artist to manage. But hopefully after a month or two, I'd have enough saved up to afford a place of my own, maybe in Duluth. It would be cheaper there than in St. Paul, but a little more urban than Runde.

Just a couple of months, I promised myself as I locked the back door behind me and walked to my car. A couple of months to get my feet under me. That's all it would be.

So why did I feel like I'd just sealed my fate?

CHAPTER 2

It took longer than I thought it would at the realtor's office. Then I stopped by the diner where I had been waiting tables since I was sixteen to pick up my last paycheck. I guess I had always known that was going to take longer than I had planned for. There were cards and cake and so many happy yet tearful hugs.

By the time Mjolner and I hit the road, it was already long past lunchtime. And despite the bellyful of cake, I stopped at Tobies when I was passing through Hinckley to grab a turkey sandwich on a toasted cranberry English muffin. Because stopping at Tobies when you're heading up north is not optional.

At least the Volkswagen wasn't making any funny noises beyond the rattle that was always there. I have no idea what is rattling or where, but I know I don't hear it when I turn up the radio. The Volkswagen had been my parents' car when they were first married, and they had driven it to Seattle and back more than once, but that had been decades ago. Lately, it was a rare day that it went as far as Minneapolis and mostly never ventured more than a few blocks from our house in St. Paul.

It groaned a bit as we climbed the last hill before reaching Duluth, and I did start to worry that it couldn't handle it.

But then we were over the top, and there was Duluth spread out before us. And beyond Duluth, nothing but Lake Superior for as far as the eye could see.

It looked cold. It pretty much always looks cold. Even now, with the setting sun lighting it up in bands of silver and gold, it radiated a warning. Don't fall into me. I'll suck the breath from your lungs before your head even goes under. I will pull you down to my coldest depths, where the light never, ever reaches.

So yeah, not exactly a friendly place. But I kind of loved it.

I hit Duluth's evening rush hour traffic, and the map on my phone kept recalculating my travel time every time I stopped at a traffic light or waited behind someone who needed to make a left. But once I was north of the city the road ahead opened up and the drive was more pleasant. To the left of me were trees, all in the full riot of autumn color. Back home, only a few maples had started turning, but just a few hours' drive north, and everything was scarlet and crimson and gold.

To my right, I could nearly always see the lake. Sometimes there were trees between me and it, but usually, I had a clear view. My mind that had been in a turmoil since saying good-bye to all my friends at the diner quieted again, even when the sun slipped behind the hills, and the waters were once more that forbidding steely gray.

I think I had gone out on it once as a kid. It must've been on a fishing vessel of some kind, but when I tried to bring up the memory, it kept getting twisted up with a drawing I had once done of Vikings on a ship. I've always loved to draw, and I loved to draw pictures that told epic stories, but I didn't remember having such a hard time telling fact from fiction. Even as a kid, I wasn't *that* imaginative.

Maybe I could've sorted out just what I did remember, but the phone kept interrupting my thoughts, making corrections to the projected arrival time. I glanced down at its screen, but the route in green hadn't changed. Runde was on the shore of Lake Superior, and everything in Minnesota on the shore of Lake Superior was on highway 61. It was impossible to get lost, really. And yet even as I looked at it the time changed again, from twenty minutes to forty-five.

Was there some inexplicable snarl of traffic up ahead in Grand Marais or something?

Was I even going as far north as Grand Marais?

I actually didn't know. When I had put my grandmother's address in the search field back at the diner it had laid out a long green line that stretched from where I was in St. Paul to a spot somewhere north of Duluth, and I had looked no closer since that was clearly the right direction.

I could back out of the directions and zoom out on the map to see where I was going, but I really hated doing that stuff when I was driving. The car wasn't the only thing that was only used to driving a few blocks away from home. Since my mother and I shared the car, I had walked or taken the bus half the time I needed to go somewhere. The highway had been less nerve-wracking than I had feared, but I could feel myself getting tired, my brain starting to fatigue from the monotonous yet not automatic activity of driving.

Yep, definitely not the time to start messing about with my phone.

But how far north *was* Runde? I tried to remember the ride up to it, or back from it, when I was a kid, but came up with nothing. Had I been there more than once? I thought I had. But I wasn't even sure if my parents had dropped me off or my grandmother had picked me up or what.

Then I saw something in front of me: lots of signage and some flags then a line of cars with the brake lights glowing red. I quickly hit the left turn signal and pulled off in a parking lot for some kind of tourist shop and general store wrapped into one.

I turned off the engine and then looked at Mjolner, who was still sitting in the passenger seat on top of all of my old art projects, gazing fixedly ahead through the windshield.

"That was the border," I told him. "I really don't think this place is in Canada."

Mjolner ignored me.

I took my phone out of its dashboard holder and realized the navigation had stopped. Great. How long had I been driving with no guidance? Had I bumped it when I was trying to look at it earlier? I went back to the search field and put the address in again, but this time it couldn't even tell me where this place was. It kept changing its mind, the map zooming in and out as the location dot changed position.

I had never seen it do this before.

Finally, I backed out of that app and scrolled through my contacts until I found my grandmother's name. I hesitated with my thumb hovering over the call button. I was pretty sure this number was hers. It had been written in blue ink in my mother's tattered old address book, but it's not like it would've changed. My grandmother hadn't moved, ever.

Unless she had gotten a cellphone? But I didn't think so. When she had tried to reach me, she had called the landline. And I know I had sent her my cellphone number months ago when my mother first started taking a turn for the worse, so we could be in touch when the end came.

But she hadn't given me a new number when she'd mailed the letter. This was all I had to try. I pushed the call button and crossed my fingers.

It rang more than seven times before it was picked up. Or maybe knocked over; at first, all I could hear was the sound of a room full of people all talking and laughing and occasionally roaring in good cheer. If this was a landline, my grandmother had taken to hosting epic parties since the summer I had spent with her.

"Hello?" I said when no one closer to the phone spoke. "Is anyone there?"

"Yeah," someone said. A man, older by the sound of it. Even with that one word, I could tell he was a northern local and definitely not from the Twin Cities. It was a very unhurried syllable.

"I'm looking for my grandmother?" I said, speaking louder since it seemed he might have a hard time hearing me over the cacophony around him.

"Who?"

"Mormor," I said, then winced. "I mean, Nora. Nora Torfa."

"Oh, yeah," he said, then dropped the phone with a clatter that had me holding my own phone a little further away from my ear.

Several minutes passed. I could still hear the sounds of a party, but one voice emerged from the general din. My grandmother, shouting orders it sounded like, but I couldn't make out the words. The phone receiver was picked up with another loud rattle of noise, but no one spoke into it. I was starting to worry that I was about to be hung up on when I heard the sound of a door closing, and the party sounds were finally muffled.

"Ingrid?" my grandmother said.

"Mormor," I said. "Are you having a party?"

"What?" she asked.

"Never mind," I said.

"Where are you?" she asked.

"Um," I said, looking around. "Grand Portage?"

"Why are you in Grand Portage?" she asked.

"Because if I go any further north, I'll need a passport," I said.

"Why are you trying to get into Canada?"

"I'm not," I said. "I'm trying to get to you, but I think my phone is going crazy."

"Well, of course, your phone is going crazy," she said. I took a deep breath. This technophobic thing was going to be hard to work around.

"Look, I didn't even see any road signs," I said, although that might have been because I had been spending so much time looking at the lake and trying to remember things. But I didn't say that part out loud.

"Of course you didn't, letting your phone lead you around by the nose," she said. "I told you already; you have to use the map I sent you. Don't you still have it?"

"Yes, I still have it," I said, looking around the packed interior of the car. "Somewhere in here with me."

"Just follow the map, and you'll be fine," she said. "I have to get back out there, but I'll expect to see you within the hour. Follow the map. Then come find me in the meeting hall."

Then I was just holding my phone, listening to a very rudely loud dial tone. I tapped the hang-up button.

"Mjolner, do you know where I stuck mormor's letter?" I asked. Mjolner was washing his ears, but he paused in the motion to flick a paw against the glove compartment. I opened it up. The letter in its envelope was there resting on top of the remains of my mother's meager cassette collection.

Surely that was just a coincidence, his little paw flick. Although with Mjolner, it was a little hard to tell. I mean, I had given up doubting that he could walk through walls. "Thanks," I said.

He gave me a little mew, took one last swipe over his left ear, then slipped down off the seat to get back inside the transport crate jammed in front of the passenger seat. Not that that was even possible; the crate door was closed and pressed tightly against the front of the seat. But, like I said, he could get in or out of anything by some kind of feline teleportation.

Still, his wanting to be inside of something was weird. I mean, besides a room I went into and shut the door. Especially not his crate; he hated that thing.

I started the car and put the phone back in its holder, although I left the screen off. I looked at my grandmother's map, and for a moment, I was transfixed.

Neither of my parents could draw more than stick figures, and I had thought my skills an anomaly, but clearly I had gotten them from my grandmother. The edge of the lake was shaded so that it looked like it came up out of the page in 3D, the waves so close to moving before my eyes. The trees were identifiably autumn trees, a neat trick to pull off when all you're working with is black ink. And I should know; that's my preferred medium as well.

The road was clearly marked, and a few buildings were clustered around a crossroad. A restaurant on one corner, a gas station on the other, some undefined boxy building across from them, but nothing but tufts of grass on the fourth.

No roads were labeled, but I was sure I would spot the crossroad if I kept my eyes open and not on the lake this time.

Then I looked out the windshield and saw that not only was it full dark now, there was also so much fog blowing in it looked like I had decided to park on a Gothic horror movie set. One where the crew had gone to town with the dry ice.

This was going to get tricky.

I pulled out of the parking lot and started going back south. The lake was on my left now, but I couldn't see it through the fog. The hills of trees on my right were just as obscured. There was nothing but the road ahead of me, the stripes on the pavement reflecting my headlights back to me, the hypnotic swirls of cloudy fog parting to let my Volkswagen through.

Then I passed through a little town, not the one on my grandmother's map, but it heartened me all the same. I had seen the buildings through the wisps of fog, enough to know they weren't the buildings I was looking for. So this mission wasn't impossible.

But as minutes started becoming ever larger fractions of an hour, my heart sank again. I was driving more slowly south than I had going north, but still. I was going to end up back in Duluth, knowing I had missed Runde again. At that point, I would just have to dip into my savings and get a hotel room. There was no way I was going to try driving this road again. The fog was definitely getting thicker, and my mind was edging past exhaustion.

I glanced down at the seat beside me where the letter was resting. I had left it open, but it had tipped away from me, and I could no longer see the map. But there had been other landmarks sketched out on it. I should at least be able to tell if it was south of Grand Marais or north of the Splitrock Lighthouse or something. Some clue if I had gone too far.

I reached over to tip it back my way. I swear I only glanced away for a second, but in that second, everything changed.

I mean, like, the entire world. The fog had pulled me out of my normal time, or pulled something from the past into my time, or something.

Anyway, he was there, right in front of my car, larger than life. I don't think I even got a proper look at him before I pulled hard on the wheel to swerve out of the way.

My brain wouldn't make sense of it. I had only one thought. Or more of a question.

Was that really the Norse god Thor standing in the middle of Highway 61, his long red-gold hair and beard streaming wildly in a sudden wind, with a sword and an ax hanging from his belt, thrusting a spear out at me like a cross guard giving me a firm warning to give his wards the right of way?

Or was it just some random red-haired Viking?

Because seeing the Norse god Thor in the flesh in that moment somehow felt way crazier than just seeing a Viking not of the football-playing kind.

But that question was just a flash of thought. The instant I tried to swerve, my only thought was that the fog had made the road slicker than it looked, and even the slow speed I had been driving through the fog was far too fast to dodge around this spear-wielding warrior in time.

I jerked at the wheel, felt the tires hydroplaning over the pavement, and my back end started fishtailing. I went sideways for a moment, a long sickening moment where I feared I was going to start rolling end over end. From the widening of his eyes, I think the Viking thought so too, in that brief moment when I skidded past him.

Then I caught a glimpse of something else: a woman's body sprawled across the highway's centerline. She looked like a rag doll dropped to the ground, her long blonde hair fanning out all around her face, covering it from view.

Then I straightened the car back out and tried braking again. I saw the tree, far too late. I watched in slow motion as the front end of the trusty old Volkswagen crunching up like an accordion. There wasn't much front end to smash before everything reached me inside the car.

But then everything just went black.

CHAPTER 3

I was never entirely out of it, I don't think, but I wasn't entirely *there,* either. My memories of those first few minutes are like they were printed on glass and then shattered, just jagged fragments that were missing key details. You could try to put them back together, but they didn't quite fit.

I remember brushing windshield glass out of my hair. It seemed important at the time, to get all of that out before I even tried to get out of the car. I don't know why. Already I could feel the growing goose egg on my left temple and was careful not to touch it in my glass-brushing efforts.

I remember the tree branch that had speared its way through the windshield like a knight's lance, coming to a rest mid-thrust through the space between the two car seats.

At first, I couldn't hear anything but the ringing of my own ears, muffled as if the cottony fog had penetrated my very skull.

Then there were voices all around me, and hands reaching for me, but I couldn't get my eyes to focus on anything. I tried to slap the grabbing hands away, but they were persistent, tugging and pulling at me. Then there was a click as someone finally unbuckled my seatbelt, and I was pulled out of the car.

And then I promptly fell to my knees on the wet grass. I didn't puke, but I really wanted to. All I could do was hold on with both hands to the crabgrass that grew on the side of the freeway, just holding on as the whole world kept spinning, and not in a fun way.

Then I remembered my cat.

"Mjolner?" I said and tried to crawl back to the car. This was complicated by the spinning and a complete lack of any idea about which way I should go to reach the car.

"What did she say?" a man asked.

"I think she means the cat," a woman said. "Look, there in the front seat."

"I've got him," another woman said, and I heard a car door open.

"Luke, help me," a different man than the first said as he slipped an arm around me and tried to hoist me to my feet. Whoever he was, he smelled really good. My mind wanted to linger in that fresh woodsy aroma, but my body kind of just wanted to melt back down into the ground. But then another arm was around me and between the two of them they got me walking. I lifted my head to look around, but my eyes were still fighting any attempts to get them to focus.

"Where?" I croaked. I couldn't get more than that one vague word out.

"We've got you," the man not named Luke said.

"Here," the second woman said, and I heard the sound of someone running over loose gravel. Then a door was squeaking open, and lights came on. I could see the doorway all lit up like a magic portal offering a way out of this world of fog and confusion and pain.

Then I was inside, and it was too bright to see anything at all.

"There's a couch in the café area over there," the second woman said. The two men walked me a little further along. They lowered me down, and I was sitting on firm cushions.

An eyeblink later, I was lying down on them. I hadn't meant to fall over, it just sort of happened. I hoped I wasn't too dirty from falling down on the grass outside. The couch under me was so firm it must have been brand spanking new, and I didn't want to ruin some stranger's new furniture.

"I brought the first aid kit from the restaurant," the first woman said, and I heard the door close behind her. "Here, take this little guy from me so I can use both my hands."

"Mjolner?" I asked, trying to squint into the light. I couldn't find him, but he meowed back at me. If he was mad at me for crashing the car with both of us in it, he didn't act like it. He didn't sound particularly concerned about me either, but then that was probably asking too much from a cat.

He had gotten into his transport crate when we'd left Grand Portage. Had he known this was going to happen?

No, that was crazy talk.

I mean, not crazier than hallucinating Vikings in the middle of the highway. Definitely not crazier than thinking I had almost hit a Norse god with my Volkswagen. But still. Crazy talk.

"Your cat is just fine, don't you worry," the second woman said.

"Wait, where did Todd go?" the man who wasn't Luke asked. "He was right here a minute ago."

"I sent him to get Nora," Luke said.

"Nora? Why?"

"Because this is Nora's granddaughter," he said as if this were plainly obvious. I never thought I looked like her much.

"Oh, right," the second woman said. "Red hair. Dead giveaway."

I wanted to say something, starting with telling them my name, but I couldn't get the words out, and the lights were still too bright, especially when someone gently brushed away the hand I was using to shield them.

"Okay, this might sting a little," the first woman said, and then a warm cloth was pressed over the goose egg on my temple. I hissed in a breath, but the pain actually wasn't too bad.

I tried opening my eyes again and could, with great effort, focus on the faces around me so long as I did it one at a time. They all looked about my age, so mid-twenties. The woman squatting beside my head on the couch had honey-brown hair pulled back in a ponytail and was wearing the sort of polyester uniform I had worn when I had waited tables back at the diner in St. Paul. Her name tag said MICHELLE.

The woman leaning over her shoulder with Mjolner in her arms had blonde hair in braids that wrapped around her head like a crown. She was wearing overalls over a tank top and had tons of flecks of paint all over her clothes and skin both. Once I saw it, I became instantly aware of the smell of fresh paint in my nostrils. Very fresh. Like the whole room around me had just gotten a coat, and it wasn't even dry yet.

The two men were standing together at the other end of the couch, watching Michelle dabbing at my head with their arms crossed. The one in front had dark blond hair and was wearing a fisherman's sweater covered with little bits of sawdust and thin curls of wood. He was the one I had smelled before, then. The scrunch of his shoulders and the way his eyes kept wincing as Michelle wiped away the last of the blood on my head and gently laid a wad of gauze over it spoke of real empathy.

But the guy behind him with hair in sinfully thick waves of chocolate brown? He was clearly crossing his arms in imitation of the first guy, scrunching his shoulders the same way. But his flinches were a fraction of a second later than the blond guy's, and he never stopped smirking. I realized he had been waiting for someone to notice him there, mimicking the other fellow's stance, and I quickly looked away. No need to reward that sort of childish behavior.

But someone was missing. Someone who ought to be there. And I didn't think it was anyone named Todd.

"Where's the Viking?" I asked. Michelle put a hand on my shoulder to discourage me from trying to sit up.

"What Viking?" the blond man in the sweater asked, that worried line between his brows deepening.

"I saw a Viking standing in the middle of the road," I said.

"I think she has a concussion," he said with a frown.

"You've barely started EMT classes, Andrew," the man behind him scoffed. If the blond one was Andrew, then the smirking one was Luke. Even with a head injury, I could deduce that much.

"I think he's right, though," Michelle said. "Did someone call 911?"

"I did," the woman with Mjolner in her arms said. "They're sending someone. But one of us should go out there and make sure they don't miss seeing us. Again."

"I'll go," Andrew said and turned towards the door. Watching him cross the room, I noticed more of the space around me. The couch I was on was surrounded by other new-looking pieces of furniture: deep, comfortable chairs and loveseats with assorted sizes of tables scattered throughout. But beyond that were bare shelves, several rows of them. Like I was in a bookstore or library, but someone had stolen all of the books.

Then I smelled the paint again. Okay, a new bookstore that didn't have the books on display yet. That made more sense.

Andrew opened the door, but rather than going outside, he backed up several steps to let someone else come in.

My grandmother. I knew her at once. She looked exactly the same as I remembered her, with long white hair that hung down her back in a single thick braid. She was wearing a bulky gray sweater with faded jeans and what could only be described as work boots.

These were her party clothes? I had the sudden urge to giggle, but the first few snickers that escaped me were met with several looks of alarm, and I quickly stifled the impulse.

"After midnight," Luke said, glancing at his wrist. If that statement was strange, the fact that he had no watch only made it stranger.

"What's happened?" my grandmother demanded. I thought she was talking to me, but it was Michelle that answered.

"Her car went off the road," she said. "We all heard it when she hit the tree. This was the closest place to take her, although I think we should've gone to the restaurant instead. I didn't realize Jessica was in here painting."

"It's nontoxic paint," Jessica said.

"I see lights," Andrew said as he peered down the road from the doorway.

"Go, Andrew," my grandmother said without turning to look. Then she noticed Luke still standing at the end of the couch. "Why are you here?"

"I heard the crash," he said with a shrug. The smirk was gone, but merriment still danced in his dark eyes.

"Let me see," my grandmother said, shooing Michelle out of her way. Then her face was close to mine as she examined the knot on my head.

"Hello, mormor," I said. She ignored me.

"She thinks she saw a Viking out in the road," Jessica said. I think it was meant to be a whisper, but in the empty bookshop, it carried loud and clear.

"A Viking?" my grandmother said, looking up at Luke for some reason.

"Don't look at me," he said, raising his hands as if in surrender. "You can see for yourself I'm dressed just like a normal person."

"Andrew thinks it might be a concussion," Jessica said. I was starting to agree. Half of what was happening around me made no sense, and my head was throbbing.

"I saw a man with red hair and a beard," I said, trying very hard to sound like I wasn't insane. "He was standing over a woman who was lying right in the middle of the road."

"What woman?" my grandmother asked as she looked at the others, but everyone was open-mouthed in shock. "No one else saw a woman?"

"We all ran straight to the car," Michelle said. "We didn't look for anything out on the road."

"I'll go," Luke said.

"Thank you, Luke," my grandmother said, then sat on the edge of the couch to lean over me. It was too aggressive of a movement for me, and I pulled away from her, pressing back against the cushions, not sure at first what she was doing. Then I realized she was looking at my pupils. "I think you're fine," she said. I didn't argue. My head hurt too much to try.

The yellowish glow of the overhead lights was joined by the brighter strobing lights from emergency vehicles, and the three women around me all straightened up to look out the window. I sat up to rest my chin on the back of the couch and look out the window myself. There were a couple of police cars - from the county sheriff's office, I thought, although I couldn't read what was written on the doors - and a single ambulance. The fog was as thick as ever, anything on the other side of the two-lane road lost in that grayness, but when Andrew pointed something out to the officers and paramedics, we all followed his finger and saw it too.

There *was* a woman lying in the middle of the road. I hadn't imagined that. But before I could feel too pleased with myself, I had to admit there weren't any Vikings or Norse gods out there.

Then the officers waved for Andrew to get out of the way, and he came running back to the bookshop, hands buried in his pockets. He met Luke on the way, and they both came in the door together.

"It's Lisa," Andrew said the minute they were inside.

"Lisa Sorensen?" Jessica asked, and Andrew nodded gravely. Jessica hugged Mjolner tight as she half sat down on, half collapsed into one of the puffy chairs. Then she looked up with a desperate sort of hope on her face. "Is she-?"

Luke shook his head. "Dead," he said.

"Did she... was she...?" Jessica stammered but always leaving her thoughts unfinished as she sent a nervous look my way.

"She was like that when I got here," I said. "That's why I swerved. To *not* hit her."

"I didn't see a mark on her," Andrew said. "No blood, not even any dirt. It's like she walked out there, laid down and went to sleep."

"Only she's not breathing," Luke added.

"Why would she do that?" Jessica asked. "Walk out onto the highway? She wouldn't even try to cross that road in this weather, let alone stop in the middle. What happened?"

"I'm sure we'll know more in the morning," my grandmother said, putting a hand on the younger woman's shoulder. "I should get Ingrid down to the village. Michelle, can you stay with Jessica?"

"Of course," Michelle said.

"I'm okay," Jessica said, but she didn't sound okay. Not at all. She sounded like she was about to completely fall apart. Like the grief was about to overwhelm her in a tsunami of tears.

I knew the feeling.

"Tell the police I saw a man," I said, sitting up straighter on the couch.

"A Viking?" Michelle said skeptically.

"Maybe leave that out," I said. My head ached terribly, and without thinking, I pressed a hand to my forehead then flinched when a fingertip brushed that swollen knot. "There *was* a man there. Maybe leave out what I thought he might be wearing. I must have been confused."

"You're not confused," my grandmother said. Then she turned to shoot a glare at Luke, who was standing behind her with that big grin back on his face. Why was he so amused? And why did that irritate my grandmother so much?

Actually, scratch that second question. I had been in his company for less than ten minutes, but I could already see that Luke was more of an acquired taste, personality-wise.

"We should let the paramedics look at Ingrid," Andrew said as I took my grandmother's offered hand and let her pull me to my feet.

"No, I'll see to her myself," my grandmother said.

"Wait, all of my stuff is in my car," I said.

"It's fine," Andrew said. "My father's garage is just across the street. We'll tow it inside when the police are done. Your stuff will be perfectly safe."

"We'll come back for anything you need in the morning," my grandmother said. "For now, we should get you to bed."

"Mjolner," I said. My grandmother's eyebrows went up in surprise, but then Jessica stood up and held out the cat.

"This is Mjolner," she said, managing with some difficulty to unhook each of the cat's claws from her overalls and transfer him to my grandmother's arms. "Her cat."

"Oh, I see," my grandmother said, looking over the cat's face as if she expected to find him familiar somehow. "I thought perhaps he was yours. Bookshops should have cats."

"I'll keep that in mind," Jessica said, but the smile on her lips wasn't reaching her eyes.

The minute I stepped out of the bookshop and back into that fog, it was like the fog was in my brain too. My grandmother seemed to realize it. She tucked Mjolner under her left arm so she could keep her right hand close to my elbow as she led me alongside the highway towards a bridge I hadn't even noticed before, although I must have driven across it earlier in the evening.

But we didn't cross it. Instead, we veered away from the highway and a little closer to the lake. It looked like an unbroken row of brambles in front of us, but then a path just sort of opened up before us.

I followed my grandmother down that path, but I had to keep my eyes on the ground in front of me. It was all I could do to focus on taking one step after another as the path made a zig-zag pattern down the side of a steep hill.

I could hear the rushing of a river pouring over rocks and into pools, the sound growing as we descended, but I never caught a glimpse of it. Then the path leveled out, and we were walking down a road, past some houses or buildings, their shapes only the roughest of outlines in the darkness. They had lights on them, but those lights only made glowing spheres in the fog that illuminated nothing.

Then I was going in another door, but it was like I was bringing the fog in with me. My thoughts were muddled, and I couldn't make my deadened feet move without tripping over everything. My grandmother's hand on my elbow was my only guide up a flight of narrow, steep stairs and then into a room and then at last onto a bed covered in a fluffy warm duvet.

I sank into that duvet and fell asleep at once, just sprawled face down on top of the bed like that. But my grandmother came back just a few minutes later and woke me up again.

"Drink this," she said, pressing a warm mug into my hands. I took an eager sip, expecting the tea sweetened with fresh honey that I remembered from my childhood. The memories felt closer now, although my mind couldn't hold onto any of them. But this wasn't that tea at all, and I immediately tried to push it back to her.

"Ick," I said. "Bitter." Crushed aspirin was less bitter. What was in that tea?

"Drink. You need it," she said and tipped the cup to my lips like I was a small child. "I'm not leaving until it's gone."

I sipped at the drink but couldn't manage more than small amounts at a time with a lot of wrestling with my gag reflex between sips. While I worked at it, my grandmother took off my shoes and got the duvet out from under me.

When at last the foul drink was gone, she let me fall back onto the pillows. I think I was mostly asleep before the duvet had even drifted down around me.

Then, like he always did, Mjolner climbed up onto the pillow behind my head and turned around and around before settling down, his spine pressed against the back of my neck, and began to purr.

After that, I knew no more.

CHAPTER 4

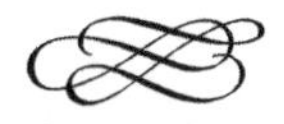

I don't know what was in the tea my grandmother had given me, but never in my life have I woken up so clear-headed and wide awake. I was super alert, and I hadn't even had any coffee yet. I reached up and pulled the bandage off my head then touched the normal contours of my temple.

It was like nothing had ever happened at all.

Except that someone named Lisa was probably still dead.

Then I remembered telling a room full of people that I had seen a Viking. I felt my cheeks flush just at the memory. That couldn't possibly have happened. What was more likely was that I had seen someone there, some hipster lumberjack type, and thinking back on it later, I had tainted the memory with the latent Norse myth imagery my brain always soaked in.

I mean, nearly everything I drew had a Viking in it somewhere. Even stuff for class assignments that wasn't supposed to. I would just slip a little Norse something hidden in a pattern like an Easter egg. It was a compulsion.

Yes, that made the most sense. My imagination had run away with me. Now that my head was clearer, I could see that.

I rolled over, but Mjolner was gone from my pillow. He usually was an earlier riser than I was. But then I looked past the indentation his body had left on the pillow, and I saw a little square window set in a deep window frame. And through that window, I could see the spindly tops of evergreen trees.

And beyond that, Lake Superior.

My secret window! Just looking through it was triggering another cascade of memories. I was back in the same built-in bed that had been mine all those years ago.

I sat up, throwing back the duvet and swinging my bare feet down to the wide planks of the wood floor. It was chilly, and I missed the wool slippers child-me had always put on straight away in the morning.

Mine was an attic room, the ceiling like an inverted V with no walls on two sides. The bed was built into the outer wall, the large rectangle that held the bed itself surrounded by cabinets of a dozen different sizes. The reddish-gold of the wood glowed in the morning light that cascaded down from the skylight that slanted above, and I ran my hand over the familiar shapes of all of the different handles and pulls on the cabinets. They were wrought iron that twisted in a variety of braids or animal shapes.

I peeked into a few, but they were all empty. Like they were waiting to be filled with everything I'd brought back from my other world. All of my stuff that was still in my car.

Stuff like clean underwear and clothes that hadn't been in a car wreck.

My grandmother had taken off my shoes and socks, but I was still wearing my jeans and sweater. I didn't seem to have any glass fragments on me, but I still felt very unclean. I wanted a shower, but I also wanted clean clothes to put on after that.

I was going to have to find my grandmother.

I stepped out of my room and out onto the balcony that overlooked the one room that was almost the entirety of my grandmother's cabin. From where I was standing, I could see the heavy timbers that supported the roof, row after row of beams carved in a twisting pattern of Nordic knotwork. I leaned over the railing to look down into the room below, but I didn't see my grandmother. The fireplace that dominated the far wall was devoid of fire, and the long table down the center of the room was bare, the benches on either side drawn neatly up beneath it.

I went down the narrow stairs that ran along the wall to my bedroom then took a left turn halfway down to hug the cabin wall. I took a turn back again, away from the main space, and into the kitchen tucked under my loft.

She wasn't there either. I could see the tea kettle sitting on the back burner, just like ours always did back home. We Torfa women like our tea. But when I touched a fingertip to its side, it was cold. So I hadn't just missed her.

I turned to look towards the fireplace again. I could see the door beside it, the one that led to my grandmother's room. Suddenly I was eight years old again, so intense was my feeling that I absolutely, positively must never open that door. Ever.

But I was a grownup now. Surely if I needed something, I could at least knock on that door?

I dithered, taking a few steps across the room but then a few steps back, not sure what to do. I had only made it halfway across the great room when the back door behind the kitchen opened with a bang, and I jumped.

"Mormor!" I said, rushing back to the kitchen as if afraid to be caught even that close to her bedroom door. My grandmother was in the mudroom shutting the door behind her, but she didn't step up into the kitchen. She was dressed like the night before, but in a different sweater and with a navy blue wool cap covering her hair.

"You're up," she said. "How's your head?"

"I feel fine," I said, touching the spot where the lump had been. "What was in that tea?"

"This and that," she said with a dismissive wave. "Your shoes and socks are right here. Put them on, and we'll go up to your car and see what you need that we can carry back down."

"Great," I said, sitting on the step between the kitchen and the mudroom to pull on my socks and sneakers. I had another rush of muscle memory from all the times I had done just this when I was a kid. "You know, I thought I had forgotten all about this place, but now that I see it again, I know that I didn't. I can show you drawings I've done that are clearly of this house. At the time, I thought I was making it up. Especially that fireplace."

My grandmother didn't answer, just glanced up at the fireplace that dominated the far side of her cabin as if trying to puzzle out what was so special about it.

"OK, ready," I said. She just nodded and stepped back outside.

The fog had turned to rain while I slept. The morning sky was clear now, but the ground was still wet. A series of flat rocks marked out a path from my grandmother's back door to the unpaved road, but the space between the rocks was moss and mud. I stepped carefully, not wanting to mess up my one good pair of sneakers. To judge by all the mud clinging to my grandmother's boots, this was bound to be a losing battle.

I expected us to turn back towards the path we had taken down the night before. I could see the bridge up there, although any sounds of traffic passing by were drowned out by the rush of the river just out of sight through a tangle of shrubs that ran alongside my grandmother's house. But she walked the other way instead, towards the lake, and I followed.

It's called the town of Runde, but "town" doesn't really describe it. If you counted up every building that made up that town, the vast majority of them would be fish houses. And those were all built right on the lakeshore, out of sight from the road. Of course, those fishermen lived in homes, but these were largely built under the cover of trees, their exteriors painted in dark colors that had a camouflaging effect. My grandmother's house next to the river was a rarity, standing rather close to the road. The bulk of its walls were also painted a dark brown, but the white trim around the doors and windows and its shutters - which were both cute and functional - made it look downright friendly.

There was only one building down here that wasn't a home or a fish house. That was the meeting hall, which was a little further up the river from my grandmother's cabin, just inland from the bridge high overhead. I remembered being there as a kid, but couldn't summon a specific image to my mind. But I had a hunch when I finally did see it, I would recognize it as yet more source material for my art.

"Good morning, Andrew," my grandmother said, and I saw the young man in question coming out of the trees between us and the lake, following a line of paving stones. His home must be back that way somewhere, but all I could see were layers of evergreen trees dotted with the occasional birch. Any house lurking in those depths was lost in the shadows.

"Good morning," Andrew said. He was wearing work coveralls like a mechanic would wear with a tan corduroy jacket over it, and a red watchman's cap pulled down over his ears. He looked me over carefully before smiling. "Good morning. You look surprisingly good."

"It's Ingrid," I said, thrusting out a hand. "I don't think I ever said last night."

"We knew who you were," he said, shaking my hand. His hand was a little rough, but strong and warm. He smelled shower-fresh but still woodsy. The dazed effect I experienced at that smell was back in full force. "So, you're feeling better?" He made a vague gesture around his own temple area.

"I am," I said. I could feel my cheeks heating but couldn't make myself stop blushing. Had he noticed me zone out just then? At least he thought it was maybe still part of the head injury. I hoped. "How's my car?"

"Truth?" he asked with a preemptory flinch as if in sympathy for a blow I hadn't even felt yet.

"Truth," I said and held my breath.

"It might cost more than it's worth to fix it," he said, "and I doubt it will ever run like before."

"I was afraid of that," I said. "I suppose it doesn't matter. Even if it were worth it to fix it, I couldn't afford it. I have no cash."

"Luckily, you won't need it while you're here," my grandmother said. "We can negotiate a deal with Andrew's father Jens to store it for now. No need to rush any decisions."

"Thanks," I said, but just the idea of being without a car was making me feel trapped. What if I needed something they didn't sell in the corner of Runde's meeting hall that functioned as a general store? What if I had an opportunity to do some work that required an in-person meeting?

What if I just wanted to leave?

My panic must have been showing on my face because Andrew was watching me with growing concern. But when he opened his mouth to say something, we were interrupted.

"Hey," Luke said as he walked up from behind me. "Ready, Andrew?"

"Yeah," Andrew said.

"Where are you two off to?" my grandmother asked, fixing them both with a stern look as if they were also her grandchildren.

"Luke and I were going up to the café to help Jessica shelve her stock," Andrew said, then glanced at his watch. "We promised to be there by eight. We better run."

"She promised us scones," Luke said.

"You're taking quite an interest in this newest commercial venture," my grandmother said to Luke.

"It could be interesting," he said with a careless shrug. "You know how I love meeting new people."

"Behave," my grandmother said, wagging a finger at him, but he just smirked.

"Always do," he said and made a swiping motion at Andrew's elbow.

"Bye," Andrew said over his shoulder to me as he was dragged away.

I had a lot of questions, but that stern look wasn't softening on my grandmother's face. It was probably safer to stay quiet and observe for a while. When I understood things better, I could start asking things. Like why everyone seemed to consider my grandmother some sort of boss around here. Was she the mayor or something?

We continued on down the road past the half-hidden homes of fishermen who had surely gone out on the water long before I had gotten myself out of bed. We occasionally saw a wife working in her yard or children too young for school playing under the trees. They would return my grandmother's waves of greeting, but they never moved closer to talk.

"I think I remember this," I said, and she gave me a quizzical look. "The aloofness."

"They aren't unfriendly here," she said. "They're just busy. Always busy. They keep to themselves and are generally quiet types, but when anyone needs anything at all, the whole community pulls together. You'll see."

"So, it doesn't bother them that the bridge is all the way up there?" I said, gesturing back over my shoulder at the bridge that was no longer in view. We had come further along the stony bluffs than I had realized. "It's up there, and the town is down here. Any hope for tourist dollars is just passing you by."

"They're fishermen, not... whoever takes money from tourists," my grandmother said.

"I didn't realize there were still independent fishermen working," I said. "I thought everything would be big corporations by now."

My grandmother shrugged, then said too quickly, as if eager to steer the conversation another way, "some of the young people think like you do about making money off the highway. Jens Swanson's grandfather built the service station decades ago, of course, and Michelle Larsen's mother Anna opened the restaurant next to it in the 80s. They do all right, being right on the highway. But Michelle has big ideas for what she wants to do when the restaurant is fully hers. After her mother retires. Modern ideas, I guess. And then there's Jessica with her new bookstore café."

"Things are changing, then?"

My grandmother just shrugged.

"Can I ask one more thing?" I asked.

"Ask anything you like," she said.

"You've been living here your whole life, right?" I asked. She nodded, but there was something guarded in her eyes. "So why do you call the people who live here 'they?' Shouldn't that be 'we?'"

Her eyes narrowed at first, but then she laughed out loud and gave a little nod. "Good catch."

"What's the answer?" I asked.

She laughed again. "I said you could ask all you like. I didn't say I'd answer." I just gaped at her, but that was too much of an invitation for the swarms of little bugs that drifted in clouds over the shady parts of the road. I shut my mouth. "Come on," my grandmother said, waving for me to follow her off the dirt road. "We're taking this path up to your precious highway. It's a little steeper than the other path, so watch your step. And don't dawdle; I'm late to get to the meeting hall already."

The minute she stepped off the road, she disappeared, as if the scarlet shrubbery had swallowed her up. Taking a deep breath, I plunged in after her.

CHAPTER 5

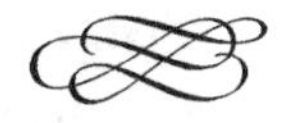

Seeing my little yellow Volkswagen, all smashed up just about broke my heart. Then I remembered that someone had actually died, so maybe I had gotten off easy with a quick-healing head injury and some property damage.

Still. My parents had left Runde together in that Volkswagen, way back before they were even engaged. That little car had been witness to so much. Like my entire life.

I would've liked to have taken a moment to process my feelings, but my grandmother's impatience was getting palpable. I dug through the trunk and the back seat, pulling out what I needed most of all, like my clothes. I had it down to bare necessities and was about to shut the car back up again when my grandmother made a tisking noise and quickly shoved half of it back in the car.

"This will be enough for you to shower and change your clothes," she said, shoving one of the overly stuffed duffle bags into my arms. "I'll carry what your cat needs."

"But-" I started to say, reaching for one of the other bags. She slammed the trunk before I could quite touch it.

"You'll thank me later," she said. "I'll help with this load, but then

I've got to get to the meeting hall. You'll have to fetch the rest on your own as you can."

I was afraid we'd have to cross the highway again. I had hated it a minute ago when we'd done it while carrying nothing at all. How was I going to attempt it this time with the bag in my arms blocking half of my vision?

But when my grandmother stepped out of the garage with the plastic crate holding cat bowls, a half-empty bag of food, a litter tray, and a mostly full bag of litter, she started walking to the far end of the service station parking lot, not towards the highway.

"Maybe we should trade," I said as I hurried to catch up. The shoes and clothes in the duffle I was carrying were bulky, but that bag of litter all on its own was quite heavy, especially for a...

It suddenly occurred to me I had no idea how old my grandmother was. In her sixties? Seventies?

"This is nothing," she said before starting down yet another steep path that zig-zagged under the bridge down to the river below.

By the time we emerged back on the dirt road, I was completely out of breath. She was right; small loads were all I'd be able to do.

"Come on," she said, pointing with the crate towards her cabin. She didn't even look out of breath. How was that possible?

Mjolner met us at the door. He moved out of my grandmother's way then blocked mine, yowling at me in a series of deeply irritated meows.

"Sorry," I said. "I'll get you food and water in just a second, okay? Stop yelling at me."

"Hopefully, it's not the litter box he was missing most," my grandmother said. I couldn't tell if she was joking or not.

I almost told her she didn't need to worry, that if Mjolner wanted to get outside, he would just walk through the walls until he was in her garden, but I bit my tongue and held the words back just in time.

"I have to get to the meeting hall," she said. "Get your cat settled in and take a shower. Leave those clothes in the cellar by the washing machine; I want to do them separately in case there is still glass in them."

"I can wash my own clothes, mormor," I said.

"Then do so," she said. "Come find me when you're ready, and I'll fix us some lunch. You remember how to get there?"

"Sure," I said. There was only one road in town and only one direction along that road we hadn't gone down yet. It ended at the meeting hall.

It was pretty much impossible to get lost in Runde.

"Good. Don't dawdle. You can make more trips up to your car this afternoon if you like," she said.

I wanted to groan out loud but mustered a smile again. By the time I had all of my things down to the cabin, I should be given a mountain goat merit badge or made an honorary sherpa or something.

After she had left, I filled Mjolner's food and water bowls and set his kitty litter down in the cellar. I put everything I was wearing in the washing machine then ran back upstairs to carry the duffle bag to my room.

I had forgotten about the smell of well water, earthy and metallic. It wasn't a bad smell, but it did bring more rushes of memory back to me. As a kid, I had been deathly afraid of spiders, and the murky depths of the cabin shower always seemed like they could hide dozens of them.

The next trip up to the car would definitely be for art supplies. I felt like I was letting all of this imagery just rush right by me, not getting any of it down on paper. But if everything I smelled, heard, or saw was going to trigger another tsunami of memories, I'd have plenty of opportunities to catch up later.

Once I was dressed with my long red hair loose so it could air dry, I made a quick pass through the cabin, just to be sure Mjolner hadn't picked some corner to use as a litter box in absentia. He followed me around, meowing at me questioningly as if he didn't know exactly what I was doing.

I checked everywhere except my grandmother's room. That door was still closed. He would've had to walk through that door to get in there, which he totally could do, but I was willing to bet if he was that desperate he would've just walked outside instead.

My hair was still damp when I put my shoes back on to go outside, but the day had gotten warmer since the morning walk when I had longed for a wool cap of my own, and I wasn't uncomfortable. I walked to the west along the dirt road, listening to the sound of the river I still couldn't quite see as it poured over rocks and into swirling pools, always in a hurry to reach the lake.

I shivered as I walked through the shadow of the highway bridge. It was cooler there, but it wasn't entirely that kind of shiver. It was like that bridge marked a boundary which I had just passed through, from one world to the next.

Which was silly, as I was still in Runde, which was far too small to contain two of anything. My imagination was clearly still in overdrive.

The road ended in the meeting hall's parking lot. It was large enough to fit several dozen cars but currently held only a single beat-up pickup truck that was parked next to the door. The truck looked like it had once been painted blue, but that had been long ago.

As I stepped from road to parking lot, I finally got a glimpse of the river itself, the water brown and foamy like nature's root beer. Despite my grandmother's admonishment not to dawdle, I found myself crossing the parking lot not to the hall but to the edge of the river. What was its name? Runde River, maybe? No, that felt wrong. I'd have to ask.

I stood at the edge, just letting the sound wash over me as well as the occasional cold cloud of spray blown up the river from the lake that sat flat and gray in the distance to my left. I could see the edge of river water that marked the top of a falls, but where the river met the lake was too far away and just a touch below the level of where I was standing for me to see it.

Then I looked to my right and had another one of those rushes of memories. I had spent a lot of time here that summer, playing near the river bank. This view was seared in my memory, the bluffs on both sides of the river that were wider near the lake but narrowed to something like a canyon deeper inland. And at the end of that gorge was a much taller falls. As if it sensed me looking at it, the falling water caught the sun and threw up a shimmering rainbow.

I had drawn this so many times. A thousand times in crayon when going to art school hadn't even yet been a dream of mine.

How had I forgotten everything? It was crazy. That summer had clearly been seminal in forming who I was, and yet until my grandmother called me, it had been nothing more than blank pages in my mental diary.

The sun went behind a cloud, and the rainbow disappeared. I lingered a few minutes longer before finally leaving the shore and heading towards the meeting hall.

This was not a bit like I remembered it. I would almost think it had been rebuilt since the last time I was here, but no one renovating a building in the 90s would've gone with such a bland 70s look. It was just a boxy building like a thousand others seen from the freeway; basically, just a pole barn with walls only thick enough to keep out the wind, the paint of no defined color that was always peeling, the neon sign a game of hangman with only half the letters guessed so far.

I stopped and closed my eyes, trying to summon up what I remembered from before, but nothing would come to me. Clearly, I wasn't in control of this process at all. Which was maddening; it was my brain, wasn't it?

I walked past the pickup truck and pushed open one of the two heavy fire doors. As gloomy as the day outside had gotten, it was still brighter than this space, and I blinked as I waited for my eyes to adjust.

As details emerged, my heart sank further. The ceiling tiles were a patchwork of water stains, the tables were all tilted at angles on wobbly legs, the plastic cushions on the chairs sporting a variety of tears and worn patches, the floor was scuffed and torn linoleum.

This was not how I remembered it at all. I tried to force a memory again, but the closest I got was something I had drawn once in pen and ink, a Viking longhouse filled with people drinking and telling tales as they waited out the winter.

Nope. Not remotely what I was looking at now.

I heard my grandmother's voice, then a man's. I looked, but I couldn't see anyone around. The chairs were drawn up neatly to the tables, and no one was manning the window where the neighbors picked up or dropped off the mail. The shelves of the general store were fully stocked but lacking in customers, and the lights weren't even on in the far corner of the room where local meetings were held.

Then my grandmother emerged from the very last place I looked, the bar. Or, more specifically, from a door behind the bar. She was carrying a wooden crate, but it was empty. The man with her looked to be in his seventies but with a full head of silver hair that had been almost too neatly combed. It looked like he had consulted a straight edge when he had combed that part, and his flannel shirt was neatly buttoned all of the way up to his neck. He was also carrying an empty wooden crate, and as they came around the counter, he reached to take the other from my grandmother.

"I can take it out to the truck for you," she said.

"No need, no need," he said. "You're busy. I can tell."

"No more than usual," she said. Then she saw me standing in the doorway. "Here's help for you. Ingrid, come over here and help Tuukka with these crates."

"Hello, Tuukka," I said as I took the crate from my grandmother's hands. "That name sounds familiar?"

"You don't remember me?" he said. He sounded so sad.

"I'm sorry," I said. Then added, "I got hit on the head last night. I think that's muddling things."

My grandmother made a harrumph sound, but when we both turned to look at her, she pretended like she hadn't. "You used to help Tuukka on his farm. He keeps bees."

"Oh," I said. Was I remembering something? Fields of clover?

Fresh honey still dripping from the comb. That I definitely remembered.

"Ah," Tuukka said happily, and I realized my thoughts were showing on my face again. "She remembers. Jakanpoika Farms. And of course, you're always welcome to visit me again."

"I remember the honey," I said. "I don't think I've had anything like it since."

"Not in the city, no," he said. "And of course, your grandmother here transforms it into the finest mead on any continent."

"Like you've been to any other continent," my grandmother scoffed, but not in a mean way.

I followed Tuukka out to his truck and helped him load the wooden crates into the back. I was just waving goodbye when I saw another car pulling into the parking lot. A car from the county sheriff's office. It pulled right in front of me into the space Tuukka had just left. I took a step back as the door opened, and the officer climbed out. He looked young, but I couldn't see any details past the hat and sunglasses. Which was probably intentional on his part.

"Ingrid Torfa?" he asked.

"That's me," I said. Apparently, everyone in this town was just going to know me on sight. But I really didn't look anything like my grandmother.

"I have some questions for you about what happened last night," he said.

"Questions?" I said. "About the car crash?"

"No," he said, scowling at me. "About the murder."

CHAPTER 6

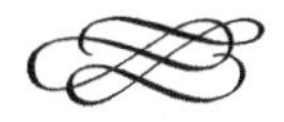

The higher functions of my brain kind of stopped at the word "murder." But the other bits were still running well enough to invite the policeman inside to talk and offer him some coffee.

The minute we were inside, my grandmother saw that I was ambling around like a head-injured zombie and brought me over to a chair at the bar. She poured coffee for me, the officer, and herself, and I took a sip before finally getting a sensible word out.

Just one. "Murder?" I said.

"What murder?" my grandmother asked.

"Hey," the officer held up his hands in mock surrender then took off his hat and glasses. He was instantly more human, just a young guy in a uniform, not a half-robot enforcer of justice or anything. "Let's start at the beginning. I'm Officer Foster from the county sheriff's office. I've just been sent to ask a few questions of Ingrid Torfa here. And you are?"

"Nora Torfa, her grandmother," my grandmother said.

"Murder?" I said again. My brain was clearly stuck on that concept.

"To be clear, you're not a suspect," he said. "I've spoken with everyone else who was at the scene last night, and it's pretty clear the victim was dead before you were even in town."

"She was lying on the road," I said. "I didn't think she was dead. I thought maybe she was sleeping. But she wasn't moving. I don't know; it all happened so fast."

"I'm sure," he said. "Did you see anything else? Perhaps on your way into town? Another car fleeing the scene, maybe?"

"No. There was no other car, at least not on the highway," I said. My grandmother was looking at me intently, like she was willing me to understand some telepathic message she was sending my way. But I had no idea what that message was. "I did see a man," I said to the officer, and my grandmother sighed then turned her attention to her coffee.

"A man?" he said.

"Yes, a big man. Like a..."

Don't say Viking. Don't say Viking. Don't say...

"Football player," I said. "Like a linebacker, maybe? Tall and muscles everywhere."

"Really," he said, his pencil poised over his notebook. "Didn't anyone else see him?"

"I guess not," I said.

"So this was outside of town?" he asked.

My grandmother was staring at me again, which was getting annoying. It was hard enough answering the policeman's questions without her glaring at me like I might get an answer wrong.

"No, he was standing over the body," I said. "I don't think I would've seen her in time if he hadn't been there. He had this spear in his hands, but across his body like this." I demonstrated, my hands curled around nothingness but showing how he had been holding the shaft of the spear. "Like a crossing guard, you know?"

"A... spear?" the policeman asked, rubbing at his head.

"Like for fishing," my grandmother said between sips of coffee. The man jumped like he'd forgotten she was there.

"And you are?" he asked.

"Nora Torfa," she said as if she hadn't already told him that.

"Ingrid's grandmother."

"Ingrid," he repeated as if trying to remember why that was familiar. Then he looked over at me. "Oh, right. Can you describe this man with a..." he consulted his notes, "spear?"

"Well, tall and jacked," I said. "With red hair."

"Like yours?" he asked.

"No, more strawberry blond. But that doesn't sound manly, does it? Strawberry blond but in a manly way," I said.

"Ginger," my grandmother said. The man jumped again. He opened his mouth to speak, but she answered before he could get a word out. "Nora Torfa. Ingrid's grandmother."

"Right," he said. "How old was this man, would you guess?"

"Thirty, maybe?" I ventured. "I'm bad at guessing ages. He had long hair and a beard, though. But not in a hipster way. More like..." any picture I had ever drawn of a Viking... "More like a... like a Viking." I had no other way to end that sentence.

My grandmother was facepalming, although if she was covering up irritation or impending laughter or something else, I couldn't tell.

"Right," the officer said, frowning at his notes. "Where was this?"

"Right over the body," I said. "Give me your notebook; I'll draw you a picture."

"No, don't do that," my grandmother said, reaching across the counter to put an arm between us before he could hand me his notebook.

"Why not?" I asked. "Why are you acting all crazy?"

"Oh," the man said, jumping yet again. "Who are you?"

"Nora Torfa. Ingrid's grandmother," my grandmother said. "I think Ingrid's told you all she can, but if you want to leave your card, we'll call you if she thinks of anything else."

"Yes. Right," the man said, blinking for a moment then standing up to retrieve a card from his wallet. It was a generic card for the entire county sheriff's office, but he turned it over to write his name and extension on the back. "You can talk to me first if that's more comfortable for you, but I'm not actually the officer in charge of the case."

"You just drew the short straw," my grandmother said. Which made no sense to me but made the officer laugh.

"Yes, actually," he said. "No one else wanted to go, but no one would tell me why. I'm actually from South Dakota; I've only been stationed here for a couple of months. Is this town supposed to be haunted or cursed or something?"

"Or something," my grandmother said, stepping out from behind the bar to walk with him back to the door.

I just sat there looking down at the half-full cup of coffee sitting on the bar in front of me. Was there something in it? Some substance that addled all our brains? Because the last five minutes had just been the strangest in my life.

And I'd nearly run over a Viking the night before.

"Officer, can you do me a favor?" my grandmother asked as she swung the door open, and a shaft of afternoon sunlight penetrated the dark interior of the hall.

"Sure thing," he said, but then added, "and who are you?"

"Nora Torfa. Ingrid's grandmother," she said as calmly as ever. "Do you have a cause of death on Lisa Sorensen yet?"

"Well, the guess is some kind of poisoning, but she hasn't been autopsied yet. We'll know more then," he said.

"Poisoning and not natural causes?" she asked.

"She may have accidentally ingested something poisonous?" he said like he wasn't sure that was the answer she had been looking for.

"The autopsy will tell you what the substance was?" my grandmother asked.

"Hopefully," he said. He tucked his notebook away and put his hat back on his head, setting it at just the right angle before adding the sunglasses. He was clearly ready to go, but my grandmother was still blocking his way.

"When you know what it was, or just have it narrowed down to a class of substances, call me," she said. Then she leaned in as if making sure that he made eye contact with her through the darkly reflective lenses of his sunglasses.

"I will," he said. "I promise."

"Thank you, officer," my grandmother said and stepped out of his way.

"I will call you as soon as I know anything," he said as he backed out of the door. "And your name is...?"

"You'll remember it when you need to," my grandmother said with a sigh that finally showed an edge of impatience to it.

"I will," he said, then touched the brim of his hat at her and at me and was gone.

"More coffee?" my grandmother asked as she came back to the bar.

"What's in it?" I asked.

My grandmother raised her eyebrows in surprise. "Are you accusing me of poisoning an officer of the law?"

"Maybe not poison, but something wasn't right," I said. "Did you drug him or something? Why was he so confused?"

"He can't help it," my grandmother said, pouring fresh coffee into her own mug and taking a long swallow despite the scalding heat of it. "He'll feel better by the time he reaches the highway. And by the time he gets back to the station, he'll remember a version of events that's a skeleton of the things he needed to know, fleshed out with everything he expected to have happened."

"Huh?" I said.

"It doesn't matter," she said.

"But it does," I said. "Is this why my memories are so messed up?"

"You're getting your memories back," she said.

"You knew that was happening?"

"Well, you keep mentioning it," she said and took another drink of coffee.

"Mormor!" I said, slamming my hands down on the bar. "Tell me the truth. Did you do something to that police officer?"

"No," she said. "You're in a sleepy town that the highway shoots right over and past without stopping. Completely forgettable. Granted, I'm sure you had no idea how quickly that happens, but still. It happens all the time. People forget Runde."

I pressed my hands to my face, trying to pull myself back together. I wasn't sure if my grandmother was serious, or crazy, or pulling my leg. And the looks she kept giving me over the rim of her coffee mug were pure inscrutability.

"I should eat," I said instead. "Didn't you say something about lunch?"

"That had been the plan," my grandmother said, setting her now-empty mug in the sink behind the bar, then pouring out the coffee at the bottom of my mug and the officer's.

"And now?"

"Now we're going to see the Sorensens," she said. "Don't worry; I'm sure by now they have more food than they know what to do with."

"Why there?" I asked as I followed her to the door.

"Because their daughter has just been murdered," she said.

"But surely they already know?" I said. "That officer seemed out of it, but someone must've told them."

"Yes, they know," she said. "Everyone knows. That's how I know they'll have food there. But we have some other questions to ask them."

"We?" I asked.

"Yes, we."

"But what are *we* going to ask them?"

My grandmother sighed and stopped walking to face me. "Look, you saw that officer. He's not unique. The others who try to come down here are going to be in the same state, if not worse."

"But why?" I asked.

"Never mind that now," she said, waving her hand around as if my question was a particularly annoying mosquito. "The point is, they aren't going to be able to figure out who did this and why. So we have to."

"Are we qualified to do that?" I asked.

My grandmother chuckled at that. "Maybe more than you know," she said. But then she took off walking so fast I could barely keep up with her let alone keep pestering her with questions.

CHAPTER 7

My grandmother wasn't wrong about the food.

The Sorensens lived in one of the houses on the lakeshore, hidden away under the trees. As we came up the front walk, I could see the fish house standing right on the rocky shore, a path worn through the crabby grass between it and the side of the house. My grandmother knocked just once then let herself in.

I realized I was standing with my mouth hanging open again when I felt that familiar sensation of small insects filling it. One flew straight back to my throat, and I coughed.

"Come on," my grandmother said to me. "Don't linger on the front step. It's rude."

"Oh, *that's* rude," I said as I followed her inside, but my sarcasm was lost on her. She bent to undo her laces and step out of her boots, and I slipped off my sneakers, which were no longer as white as they'd been that morning.

I could hear voices speaking softly somewhere in the back of the house, and someone was sniffling. I followed my grandmother into the kitchen, and that was when I saw what she had meant about the food. Every surface was covered with casseroles, their tops wrapped in foil, some with little post-it notes with warming up instructions written on them in neat cursive.

Then we were in a dining room. There were no people here either, but an array of coffee cakes were set out on the table as well as a sad-looking vegetable tray and a tiered thing stacked high with little sandwiches. My grandmother paused there to pile several of those sandwiches on a napkin and hand it back to me before continuing on to the next room.

The room ran the length of the back of the house, and the entire back wall was a series of windows that looked out over the lake. It was a stunning view even on this rather cloudy and uninspired day.

The people gathered inside were dressed much like my grandmother, in jeans designed for work and either worn old sweaters or flannel shirts. There were all standing around in their thick woolen socks. At the far end of the room to my left, a couple who looked to be in their fifties sat in a pair of chairs with everyone else clustered around them. The man had a stunned look to his face, like he wasn't sure where he was or even who he was. The woman had a wad of tissues in her hand but kept wiping her eyes on the sleeve of the old, faded cardigan she was wearing.

My grandmother moved around the room, touching arms and whispering words to the other people gathered there. The visitors were mostly women, but a few men who looked perhaps too old to fish were among them. Each person my grandmother spoke to got up from their chair and wandered back to the dining room as if suddenly finding themselves hungry. By the time she had reached the couple sitting in recliners on the far end of the room, everyone else had made themselves scarce.

"Nora," the sniffling woman said and fought her way out of the chair to hug my grandmother.

"I'm so sorry for your loss," my grandmother said. "Both of you," she said, holding out a hand for the man to grasp, which he did if briefly.

Then she sat down on the edge of their coffee table so she could see them both at once. I didn't know what I was supposed to do with myself besides eat the sandwiches, which felt completely inappropriate in that moment. These people were grieving. I wrapped the napkin around the sandwiches and put them in my sweatshirt pocket then sat down in a chair against the wall. Neither of the Sorensens even seemed to notice I was there at all.

"You'll find out who did this," Mr. Sorensen said, nodding as if agreeing with himself.

"I will," she said, catching his hand again to give it another squeeze. "You can rely on me."

"We know that," Mrs. Sorensen said. "We always know that."

"I didn't know Lisa very well," my grandmother said. "She just graduated, didn't she?"

"From junior college, yes," her mother agreed. "She was going to be a nurse. She had a job lined up in Duluth. She was so excited." Her voice cracked, and she pressed a hand over her eyes.

"She came home a lot, didn't she?" my grandmother asked.

"Every weekend," her father said. "Every break. And she's been here all summer, even though she was done with school and could've started working sooner."

"She was a good girl," her mother said, wiping at her eyes with the sleeve of her shapeless cardigan again.

"Of course we knew that wasn't about us," her father said.

"She had a boyfriend?" my grandmother guessed.

"Well," he said, sitting back further in his chair and folding his hands over his stomach. "We always assumed so. She never brought anyone around, and no one ever called the place looking for her, but she has her own cellphone, you know. And she went out a lot. With friends, she said, but still and all."

"You never met him, though?" my grandmother asked.

"We assumed he was someone she knew at school," Mrs. Sorensen said.

My grandmother turned her head ever so slightly to give me a sharp look. I hadn't made a sound. I had only been thinking, if she had met someone at school like her parents thought, when did she and her boyfriend ever go out? If she came home every weekend, when would they have found the time?

I tapped a finger to my lips, a silent promise not to make a peep, and my grandmother turned back to the other two, who didn't seem to have noticed any of that at all.

"Maybe it was someone local," my grandmother said to them.

"No, we would've met a local boy," her father said.

"Not if she were afraid you wouldn't approve," my grandmother said gently.

"You mean you think she was seeing a Nelsen?" he asked, sitting up in his chair.

"Is it possible?" my grandmother asked.

"No, she'd never," Mrs. Sorensen said, sniffling again.

"Even if she had, that wouldn't matter to us," Mr. Sorensen said. "That's nothing to do with us. The fight with the Nelsens is a farming Sorensen matter. We fishing Sorensens don't involve ourselves with it."

My grandmother looked at them both sharply. Mr. Sorensen squirmed in his chair, then pretended he was just finding a more comfortable position. Mrs. Sorensen just continued dabbing at her eyes with the wad of tissues in her hand.

"You've told me that before," my grandmother said at last. "You're sure Lisa knew you felt this way?"

"Of course she did," he said. "She was our only daughter, our only child. She had no reason to ever hide anything from us. She knew that."

My grandmother sat back, and her face softened. "I'm sure you're right."

"You're going to find who did this?" Mrs. Sorensen asked, lunging forward to grasp my grandmother's knee.

"I gave you my word," my grandmother said. "You know what that's worth."

"I do," Mrs. Sorensen said, nodding a tad too empathically. "I do."

"Lisa was close with Jessica Larsen, correct?" my grandmother asked.

"Yes. Best friends since kindergarten," Mrs. Sorensen agreed. "She was here earlier. She brought these lovely little sandwiches. Oh, dear, my manners! Are you hungry at all? Let me just-"

"No, don't get up," my grandmother said. "I didn't mean to chase your company away. I'll send them back in to sit with you. I know where to find Jessica."

She leaned forward as if about to stand up but paused and looked at me, like she thought I might have something to say.

And in that moment the bereft couple finally noticed me there. So now I had three pairs of eyes trained on me, and I had absolutely nothing to contribute.

"I'm sorry to have met you in such circumstances," I said, getting up to extend my hand to each of them. "My condolences for your daughter."

"You're Ingrid," the man said.

"Yes, I am," I said.

"You were with her when she died?" he asked.

"No, not exactly," I said. "I'm sorry. She was already dead when I got there."

"Oh," he said. As if I had just crushed his soul.

"I'm sorry," I said again, lamely.

"It's time for us to go," my grandmother said, and put an arm around my shoulders to guide me out. As if I were the bereaved one.

We put our shoes back on and started walking down the mossy front walk towards the road.

"Are we going back up to the highway, then?" I asked, sneaking a sandwich out of my pocket. "To talk to Jessica?"

My grandmother was about to answer when she suddenly froze in place. I froze too, like we were deer in a herd, and one of us had just flashed the warning of a predator approaching.

But then my grandmother just called out, "Tore Nelsen. Why are you hiding behind that tree?"

I looked around but didn't spot which tree she was referring to until a little man stepped out into view. He was wearing a clean pair of overalls, so new they still had creases in them from how they'd been folded in the store. The flannel shirt beneath it was buttoned neatly all the way up, and he had a flat leather cap in his hands that he was twisting around and around.

"I wanted to pay my respects," he said, looking down at his own toes as if my grandmother were a teacher who had just called him out on the carpet.

"From behind that tree?"

"Come on, be fair," he said, still not quite looking up at her. "You know how things are."

"I know how things are between some of your family and some of theirs, yes," my grandmother said.

"I know it doesn't involve us particularly," Tore said, coming a little closer to looking my grandmother in the eye but not quite making it. "You know I don't hold with my cousins on that score. And these are fishing Sorensens, not farming Sorensens."

"So they just explained to me as well," my grandmother said. She sounded ever so slightly amused.

"Still and all," Tore said and fell silent, staring at the ground intently.

My grandmother sighed. "It would be a good gesture if you went in there," she said. "I would personally consider it a step in the right direction for both your families. Did you bring anything?"

"I have a sack of pumpkins behind the tree there," he said, his cheeks flushing pink. "They're small, but perfect for pies."

"I'm sure Mrs. Sorensen will appreciate the gesture," my grandmother said. "Go on inside now. My granddaughter and I are quite busy."

"Oh," he said, looking up and noticing me standing there. "Ingrid."

"Yes, Ingrid," my grandmother agreed. "Go on."

"I will," Tore said and dashed behind the tree to fetch the battered grocery bag overflowing with orange gourds.

"What was that all about?" I asked as we continued on towards the road.

"Hopefully, ancient history," my grandmother said.

When we got to the road, she turned back towards the meeting hall.

"Aren't we taking the shortcut up to the freeway?" I asked, looking back over my shoulder at where the bluffs jutted out into the lake.

"We're not going up to the freeway," my grandmother said.

"But... Jessica?"

"Can wait," she said. "There's something else I have to show you first."

CHAPTER 8

At first, I thought my grandmother was going to show me something in her cabin, but she only stopped at the kitchen door long enough to retrieve two sturdy walking sticks from the corner of the mudroom.

"Where exactly are we going?" I asked as I took the stick she handed me. It had been stripped of bark and polished to a fine shine, but all the original twists and whorls of the wood were still clearly visible.

"You'll see," my grandmother said and continued up the road to the meeting hall.

But we didn't stop there either. She led me down a path between the side of the building and the bank of the river to the back patio of the hall used for outdoor seating when the nights were warmer. The picnic tables and plastic lawn chairs were all neatly stacked and covered with tarps against the back wall of the building now. In another month or so, they'd be buried in snow, forgotten until spring.

Behind the patio were a few sand pits. I had a hard time imagining the people of Runde playing beach volleyball. But there must be more young people hiding somewhere besides the four I had already met.

After crossing the sandpits, my grandmother started up a trail that seemed pleasantly walkable at first, a narrow track between friendly bushes that never tried to claw at my clothing or trip me up.

But as we walked, the gentle rush of the river to our left started to pick up volume, and I looked up to see we were approaching the end of the gorge, where the taller falls were.

Then the path shot up at a grade so steep it was nearly vertical, and I was very glad indeed for the walking stick my grandmother had given me. There were enough rocks to form a sort of staircase, but these stairs were built to the scale of a giant or troll. I could just reach a foot up to rest on the stair in front of me then hoist the rest of my body up only to do the same with the other foot, over and over again.

My thighs were on fire before we were even halfway up the bluff. I wanted to ask my grandmother again where she was taking me, but she kept striding forward like she was running on train power, never slowing. The waterfall would've made speaking at any distance impossible anyway. So I just put my head down and concentrated on climbing one step at a time.

Then suddenly, the path leveled out, and I nearly collided with my grandmother, who was waiting for me, leaning with both hands on her walking stick and grinning. Her cheeks were red, and she was breathing hard, although not nearly so hard as I was.

"Do this often?" I asked loudly. We were practically under the falls by now, and I didn't know if she could even hear me, but she just laughed. I looked up and saw the path had ended because going in the same direction had become impossible. The rocks ahead were overhanging us. A professional climber with gear or one of those skilled free climbers could probably make it to the top, but I certainly couldn't.

"This way," my grandmother said, or at least that's what I think she said. Then she turned to walk towards the falling water. I couldn't see where she was going; the path was literally narrower than her body as she walked.

And then she just disappeared. I yelped, afraid I had somehow missed seeing her fall. But then I saw the path ahead of me took a sudden turn into the side of the bluff before turning again, a zigzag that led behind the sheet of falling water.

I clung as tightly as I could to the rock wall beside me and made very sure of each step before I took it. The rocks were slick with the spray from the falling water, and if I slipped, I had no idea where I would go.

One thing I was sure of: my grandmother was crazy. How had she even found this place, let alone found a reason to keep coming back?

Then the path ahead of me opened out onto a cavern filled with the flickering light of the sun filtered through all that falling water. It was damp, and the rocks were coated with moss, but the floor of the cavern sloped away from the falls. If I tripped here, I would fall to safety, so that was something anyway.

My grandmother was waiting for me again, leaning on her staff as she watched me make my careful approach.

"It's safer than it looks," she said.

"It would almost have to be," I said, "given that it doesn't look safe at all."

She scoffed. "You weren't this much of a fraidy cat when you were a kid."

"You took me here when I was *eight?*" I demanded. "No, I don't think so. I'd remember this." I looked around at the sun dancing through the falling water and the smell of wet rock and moss that clung to the air. The crashing of the water was a constant rumble that I felt in my chest as much as heard with my ears. It was unforgettable. And yet, unlike everything else I kept encountering in Runde, I had never drawn anything like it. "How could I forget this?"

"The magic is stronger here," my grandmother said. I wanted to laugh, but her voice and the look in her eyes were both completely serious. She wasn't joking.

"Mormor?" I asked.

"Don't ask me to explain," she said. "In a minute, you won't need me to. Or at least what questions you still have will be sensible ones."

"Okay," I said, not at all sure that was going to be true. I had never felt less capable of sensible thoughts in my life. "Is this what you wanted to show me? This cave?"

"Obviously not," my grandmother said with a huff, then walked a bit further into the cavern. At the far end was a narrower passage that went deeper into the hillside. That cave took a turn almost immediately, so I couldn't see how far it went or what was on the other end, but the light that flickered over its stone walls was from a fire somewhere within. I could just smell the wood burning as I drew closer behind my grandmother.

"Which Thor is guarding?" my grandmother asked loudly as she approached the cave mouth.

"It is I," a deep voice called back, "Thorbjorn." Then I heard footsteps approaching.

"Oh, good," my grandmother whispered to me as we waited at the cave mouth. "Unless I'm very much mistaken, this is the one you saw before, and he has some explaining to do. Two birds with one stone, eh?"

I didn't really understand what she meant at first. But then the silhouette of a large man appeared around the bend in the cave, at first just a black shadow backlit by the firelight. As he drew closer, I realized the impression of size hadn't been a trick of the light. He really was a huge, hulking man, built like a linebacker.

But dressed like a Viking.

I don't know exactly how it happened, but I found myself sitting on the gritty, wet ground. Like the sight of him just switched off the power to my legs. He was real. I hadn't imagined him.

"Thorbjorn," my grandmother said. "You were out on the highway last night."

"Aye," Thorbjorn said to her, but his eyes were on me. "Why is she on the floor?"

"Beats me," my grandmother said.

"But why is she here? I thought the council agreed an adjustment period was required. In fact, you insisted on it," he said. He had an accent I couldn't quite place and spoke in a sort of sing-songy rhythm. It was similar to the usual northern Minnesota way of speaking, but also different. More direct and less folksy. He didn't linger on the vowel sounds the same way.

"I would've preferred that, certainly," my grandmother said. "But as you know, there was a death. More correctly, there was a murder."

"Murder," Thorbjorn said. "Are you sure?"

"Would I bring Ingrid here if I weren't?"

"No, I don't think you would," he said after stroking his beard in thought for a moment. "But this isn't how we agreed this would be done. The council won't like it."

"The council can take that up with me," my grandmother said. "She's one of us. She won't betray us."

"I'm not the one to convince on this matter," he said. "I'm not the skeptical one. But if I just let you through, the others will say I'm too much in your sway."

"Aren't you just, though?" my grandmother said with a wink. "Well, that's a matter easily resolved anyway. Present her with a challenge."

"It should be done in front of the entire village," Thorbjorn said. "Or at least the council."

"And yet, needs must," my grandmother said. "You were both there, with Lisa Sorensen, near her end."

"All right, then," he said. "Come back to the fire. We can do it there."

He turned to walk back down the narrow cave, and my grandmother reached out a hand to help me back to my feet.

"Challenge?" I asked her.

"Don't worry. You'll pass. You're my granddaughter," she said.

"But what do I have to do?" I asked.

"Just remember what I've always taught you," she said. "Calm your mind, and the answers will come."

"This is a test with answers?" I all but squeaked.

"You would prefer a feat of strength?" she asked, and yet again, I couldn't tell if she was joking or what.

I followed her down the hall to a smaller cavern completely dominated by a roaring bonfire. It lit up the space and dried out the air, but almost too much. I could feel my hair crackling as the mist from the waterfall evaporated all in an instant. I looked up, but the top of the cavern was lost in shadows. Somewhere up there had to be some sort of chimney, or this place would be filled with choking smoke.

"Here," Thorbjorn said, setting a three-legged stool close to the fire and gesturing for me to sit there. Now that I could see him in better light, I knew for sure he was the one whom I had seen out on the highway standing over Lisa's body. He was still wearing the same wide belt, but the weapons no longer hung from it. I looked around then saw them leaning against the cavern wall within arm's reach of the largest of the stools.

I hadn't expected Vikings to smell so good. Sort of outdoorsy, but clean. And if the wool cloth his clothes were made from was homespun, it was really first-rate homespun.

Thorbjorn went over to a small wooden chest near his weapons and dug around for a bit before returning with a leather cloth that he spread out on the ground at my feet. Then he started rattling something in his hand. I could see a wooden cup through his fingers, but something was rattling around inside it. He kept looking right into my eyes as he shook the cup, like he was waiting for me to do or say something, but I had no idea what.

Then my grandmother struck the rocky ground with the end of her walking stick, a loud crack that echoed through the cavern, and Thorbjorn bent to spill a bunch of wooden staves from the cup all over the leather cloth. They fell in a messy jumble making spiky patterns that seemed to dance in the light from the bonfire.

"Well?" he said, sweeping a hand as if inviting me to partake of those bits of wood.

"What do I do?" I asked him. Then I heard my grandmother tisk. "You want me to see something," I guessed. He said nothing, but I saw the nervous glance he shot my grandmother.

I was failing their little test.

I leaned forward, resting my hands on my knees, and tried to ignore the way my skin felt instantly like it was sunburned from sitting too close to that fire. I guessed that was part of... whatever this was.

I could see the jumble of staves wasn't just random. Some had fallen in distinct patterns that sort of looked familiar.

They were runes. I knew runes, but the sudden rush of excitement when I figured that bit out turned into an even more sudden crash as I remembered I had never actually studied any of their esoteric meanings. You could use the runes as letters to write words, which I did all the time in my illustrations. You could overlap those letters to make one shape that said many things at once. I particularly loved that trick. All of my art is full of things that are more than they seem at first glance.

But never having much interest in fortune telling, I had never paid any attention to that aspect of the runes. They all were supposed to mean something, and in patterns, they meant something more. But I didn't know a thing about it.

Yep. I was totally going to fail this test.

Thorbjorn stepped away, then settled himself down on his own large stool, also sitting with his hands on his knees as he waited. My grandmother remained standing, leaning on her walking stick as if she were prepared to stay just like that all day if need be.

It was subtle but heartening. They weren't giving up on me. They were giving me more time. And they both looked like they were willing to wait forever if that's what it took. I couldn't let them down.

I looked at the shapes again and let go of my thoughts. Which sounds easy, but my brain kept trying to summon up everything it *did* remember about Norse runes, which was exactly what I needed it not to do in this moment. So it took a while. But I just kept breathing and quieting my thoughts, over and over, until they finally stopped coming back.

And then the quieter, submerged feelings could finally, slowly but surely, bob to the surface of my mind.

"Two forces," I said, pointing at different clusters of staves as if I really knew what I was talking about. "One a force that longs for motion, one that longs to be at rest. They are swirling like a maelstrom, and there is something at the center that wants it both ways. But it will have to fall one way or the other. It hasn't yet. Or rather it didn't; maybe this is in the past."

"The past?" my grandmother prompted in a whisper. I didn't look up from the shapes that were swimming before my eyes now. But surely it was the firelight making it look like the staves were dancing.

"The center is gone," I said, although I didn't know myself what I meant. "I see another pattern here," I said, moving my hand to a different corner of the cloth. "Love in its purest form, and love in its most selfish form, and at its center: death."

Then, just like that, the swimmy feeling was gone. I was just looking at slips of wood and making stuff up. I sat back on the stool and wiped the sweat from my forehead. "Wow. What was that?"

"That was what we needed to see," Thorbjorn said, then got up from his own stool to gather up the wooden staves and the cloth and put them back in his chest.

"Really?" I asked. "How do you know I didn't just make all that up?"

"Did you?" my grandmother asked me.

"I don't know," I said honestly. "But if I passed your test, does that mean you'll tell me what's really going on here? Like to start, why is there a Viking living behind the waterfall, and how come everyone in Runde thinks I'm crazy when I mention him?"

"A Viking?" Thorbjorn said.

"Well, you're certainly dressed like one," I said. "Maybe not completely authentically," I added. "You're doing some sort of modern mashup version or something."

Then I realized he hadn't said a *Viking*. He had said *a* Viking.

"Wait," I said as he chuckled to himself. "How many of you are there?"

"Ingrid," my grandmother said to catch my attention. "How much did your mother teach you of the old tongue?"

"Norwegian? Just some songs I can sing without really knowing what I'm saying," I said.

"That's it?" She sounded disappointed.

"I took German in high school, if that helps," I said. "But it probably won't. I don't think I remember any of that now."

"Everyone can speak English," Thorbjorn said. "She'll be fine."

"I suppose you're right," my grandmother sighed. "Well, come on, then. It's time for you to see where you really come from."

CHAPTER 9

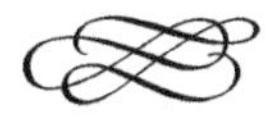

Before we left the cavern with the bonfire, Thorbjorn walked back around the bend in the cave that led towards the waterfall. I couldn't see what he was doing, but I could hear the sound of stone grinding on stone. I shot my grandmother a quizzical look.

She shrugged, "he can't just leave it open when he's not here to guard it," she said.

"There's a door?" I asked. Thorbjorn came back out. He put his sword and his ax on his belt and picked up his spear.

"Shall we?" he asked.

"Lead the way," my grandmother said.

He nodded then started walking towards the shadows on the far side of the cavern. I followed beside him, my grandmother just behind us.

Then, the moment Thorbjorn stepped out of the cavern onto a narrow cave that was stepped up like a natural staircase, the flames behind us flickered out. I looked back, but my grandmother was right there behind me. I could see her face reflecting the dim sunlight that reached us from the top of that stair.

"Let me guess, you can't just leave a fire burning with no one there to guard it," I said to her.

"Smart girl," she said, but waved for me to turn back around and start up the staircase.

Thorbjorn was so wide I couldn't see a thing beyond him until we were suddenly out in the sun, standing in a meadow of grasses that was divided in the middle by the stony banks of a river. I turned around to see the edge of where river became falls, and then far beyond that and as far as the eye could see the steely blue waters of Lake Superior.

I walked closer to the edge, where the dry autumn grass hung over the rocky edge of the bluff. I could see the gorge opening up beneath me, mostly filled with trees but dotted here and there with small farms. A creek ran at an angle first alongside and then into the river, crossed at the midpoint of what I could see by a bridge that looked like it joined two of the little farms.

I saw the roof of the meeting hall, and my grandmother's cabin, and all of the fish houses along the shore. The fishermen's homes were all tucked away under the tree cover. On beyond that, I could see boats out on the water of the lake, and even a couple of cargo ships way out by the horizon heading into or out from Duluth.

"Wait a minute," I said, my eyes tracking back to the meeting house. I knew I didn't have my geography wrong since it was the only large building on the river, but that wasn't the building I had walked past just a few minutes before. This was a large timber-framed structure, the support beams jutting out from under the thatched roof. It was too far away for me to see, but my memory filled in the details of the animals that were carved into the ends of each of those beams. "Mormor?" I said, pressing a hand to my forehead.

"It's all right," she said to me. "It will all come back, but not all at once. Just let it happen."

"I was here. When I was eight," I said. Then I turned and looked at Thorbjorn. Apparently, there was something a tad aggressive in my eyes or in my posture because he actually fell half a step back. "I remember you!" I said, jabbing a finger at him. "I remember when you were just a kid. Wait. I'm remembering *five* of you."

"My brothers," he said. "I'm the middle of five."

"The Thors," I said, remembering what my mother had said back in the cavern. Which Thor is guarding? That made sense now. He and his brother all had names that started with Thor. I couldn't quite remember them at the moment, but they were all dancing on the tip of my tongue.

"Let's walk to the village," my grandmother said. "Sadly, we are here on business, or else we could dawdle all we liked."

I laughed at that. I'm pretty sure the amount of dawdling my grandmother liked was too small to be measurable by existing technology.

My grandmother led the way through the grasses that scraped together in the autumn breeze. I followed behind her, wondering how colorful all of the flowers around me would have been just a week or two earlier. Even dried, they were gorgeous.

"Ingrid," Thorbjorn said, "I need you to promise me you won't leave the edges of the village. Don't go further than the last house in any direction."

"Why not?" I asked.

"It's not safe for you there. Not yet," he added hastily. "When your memory returns, you'll know why and can judge the risk for yourself. But even then, I'd prefer if you check with me before you decide what's safe and what isn't."

"Okay," I said. We reached the end of the meadow and were back under the cover of birch trees, their leaves spinning wildly in the wind in hypnotic patterns. Being under them was like being inside of some immense rattling toy.

"I know we broke that rule all the time as kids," he went on. "But we're not kids anymore. There are things out there, dangerous things with boundaries a wise person will respect."

"I promise," I said. I was about to ask if that was why he always went about with three weapons on him when the trees abruptly ended, and our path was now a cobblestoned road between surprisingly modern-looking houses. The walls were long vertical planks of wood of different types stained in a variety of shades, and they nearly all had a boxy design with flat roofs. They were staggered along the road, so no building on the south side was blocking the southerly view of its neighbors on the north side, and I could see why. Every south-facing wall was dominated by windows. Glass windows. And there were metal fixtures, understated ones but definitely thoroughly modern.

But the people were dressed like Thorbjorn, in clothes that looked like some fashion house decided to do a Viking-inspired line but with modern materials and construction methods. The styles and patterns and colors were like things I'd seen in the thousands of books I'd used for reference in my own illustrations, but nothing had a rough homespun look to it.

Most of the women had thick rings of keys hanging from their belts and also what I guessed to be sewing kits, although the scissors gleamed so brightly I knew these were intended to be decorative rather than merely functional.

And all of the men carried weapons. There were swords, axes, and spears like Thorbjorn carried as well as knives of various sizes and even a hammer or two.

"What is this?" I asked, and realized that once again I was sitting on the ground. "Where am I?"

"Villmark," my grandmother told me. "On the banks of the Konallelva River."

"We've been here for centuries," Thorbjorn said, "and we'll be here for centuries more."

"But this is crazy," I said, waving my hands around to take in the whole scene around me.

"What's crazy?" Thorbjorn asked, frowning as he too looked around but saw nothing that was, to him, out of the ordinary.

"First of all, Vikings never settled on the North Shore," I said. "That's a historical fact."

"We're a side step out of history here," my grandmother told me.

"It's probably better if you get used to the idea that a lot of your questions are going to be answered with the word 'magic.'"

"So wait," I said, holding up a finger to delay my grandmother when she bent to help me back to my feet. I still needed the ground beneath me for another minute. "Does that mean the Kensington runestone is *real*?" I asked.

My grandmother scoffed. I half expected her to spit on the ground, so strong was her contempt.

"She doesn't know better yet," Thorbjorn said to her.

"That stone is a fraud," she told me. "Everyone knows it's a fraud. But if you believe it's real, I have some Dare Stones I'd love to sell you." Then she took a deep breath and calmed herself. "Look, people like interesting things. And there are always people who are very good at creating interesting things to sell to those first people. Although a hoax that's been around for nearly a century becomes its own sort of history. Some of those Dare Stones are quite well crafted. But, alas, not real. And neither is the Kensington stone." Then she mumbled under her breath, "if you're going to fake something, at least get your grammar right."

"Our ancestors came here centuries ago fleeing a great threat," Thorbjorn told me. "They came here to hide, and we remain in hiding too."

"From what you warned me about that lies outside the village?" I asked.

"There are many threats. Some larger than others," he said. But I could see him trading looks with my grandmother and knew they were gaging how much to tell me and how much to hold back. I was starting to get a little annoyed with all the secrecy.

Not that I couldn't see their point. Explaining every little thing to someone who was going to remember on her own in her own time would be a little frustrating. But it was frustrating on my end too.

"Listen," my grandmother said, putting her hand out again. I took it this time and let her pull me to my feet. "You remember why we're here?"

"To not talk to Jessica?" I ventured. "You never actually said more than you wanted to show me something."

"Fair enough," she said. "Lisa's parents knew she was seeing someone. They thought it was someone at school, but we both knew that didn't make any sense, right?"

"She came back here every chance she could," I said. "I mean, to Runde."

"No, she came here," my grandmother said. "There are a few inhabitants of Runde who venture up here. And a few Villmarkers that go down to Runde. I'm not sure which happened first in the case of Lisa and her man."

"Don't you know who he is?" I asked.

"Not yet," she said. "But we'll know soon enough. A secret is only a secret until I have a need to know it."

I really wanted to ask her what she meant by that, but I was distracted when the crowd that had been slowly building a respectful distance away from us suddenly fell silent. It was like walking in the woods, and all of the birds just stopped singing at once. Eerie. Then the crowd parted to make way for a woman who was walking up the middle of the cobblestoned road.

She certainly was eyecatching. She had thick blond hair that cascaded around her in curls and tendrils like a living thing. It fairly made my fingers itch with the desire to sketch her, that hair. She was dressed all in snowy white and walked with an exaggerated roll of her hips punctuated by the metallic rattle of the keyring on her belt. From a distance, I thought she was about my age, but when she drew closer, I saw subtler signs of age around her eyes and the corners of her mouth. She was still an attractive woman, but I would put her at closer to forty than thirty.

Then she turned her gaze from my grandmother to me, and the sun hit her hair. She blazed golden, and her green eyes flashed brightly, and I would swear by all that I loved in this world that she was in her prime, young and fertile. And so very attractive; she was like a magnet pulling at me.

Then she turned back to my grandmother, and I staggered back.

Thorbjorn caught my elbow, and when I looked up at him, there was laughter in his eyes. I pulled him far enough away for us not to be overheard as the woman spoke with my grandmother in what I gathered was Norwegian.

"I just had the strongest urge to have babies with this woman," I whispered to him. "What on Earth does that mean?"

"Halldis has a bit of skill with magic," he told me. "Being young and beautiful is her particular thing. She's been doing it for decades."

"Decades?" I said. "How old is she really?" I looked at her again. She looked different while she was speaking with my grandmother. The fine lines around her eyes gave her a distinguished look, and there was silver in her blond hair. Her body language was different as well. She exuded competence and wisdom.

"I think fifty, but who knows?" he said. "She's been trying to get your grandmother to take her as an apprentice since your mother left home. She probably hit you with her full power just to prove a point."

"To me?" I said. "I'm no competition for her. I've never learned anything about magic. I didn't even know it was real less than an hour ago."

"To your grandmother," he clarified. "But I wouldn't worry about it. If she tries to make it a competition, that's exactly the wrong way to get on Nora Torfudottir's good side. And Halldis knows it. She'll cool it."

"I hope so. That was seriously weird," I said.

My grandmother turned away from Halldis, who gave me one last inscrutable look up and down before turning to stroll back up the road the way she'd come. My grandmother sighed and gave a little shake of her head, as if their conversation had been an irritation she hadn't needed.

"Did she know anything?" I asked.

"I didn't ask," my grandmother said. "It would be better to take it up with the council first anyway. They'll appreciate the gesture."

"Your grandmother likes to let them pretend they're in charge," Thorbjorn whispered in my ear, and I put a hand over my mouth to cover my laugh. My grandmother scowled at both of us.

"This is a serious matter," she said. "I'm afraid they're going to insist on not speaking English for your benefit, even though they all do so fluently. Just nod along and let me do all the talking. Now let's go."

We started walking up the cobblestoned road, past the crowd of people who greeted my grandmother and Thorbjorn but only stared at me, the strange new thing in their town.

I ignored them, looking instead at the houses around me. They had fenced-in yards, but they weren't tall fences. I could see the carefully laid-out gardens, now in the process of being winterized just like we did in St. Paul with lots of mulch and upside-down buckets to protect the more delicate plants from the ravages of a Minnesota winter. I looked inside every window, catching glimpses of rooms that looked like spreads from an Ikea catalog.

I was so busy staring at everything that it wasn't until I nearly walked into the side of a well that dominated the square at the center of town that I realized I had lost sight of my grandmother and Thorbjorn. Had they continued on straight ahead or taken one of the other options?

I looked down each road for any sign of something that looked like a council building or a meeting hall or something, but it was nothing but houses and gardens as far as I could see.

Then I saw someone sitting on the edge of the well as if waiting for me to notice him. It was Luke. But he wasn't wearing the jeans and flannel shirt I had seen him in last. No, he was dressed just like every other inhabitant in Villmark.

"Ingrid Torfudottir," he said with a wide grin. "Are you lost in your own hometown?"

CHAPTER 10

"Luke," I said.

"Actually, it's Loke," he said, brushing off the back of his pants as he got up from her perch on the stone wall of the well.

"Loki?" I said.

"No, Loke," he said, enunciating the vowels carefully. "Luke is my name for when I'm down there cosplaying as a normie."

"Still, you're named for the trickster god, right?" I said.

"First of all, my parents named me that when I was born," he said. "Secondly, do you expect every guy you meet who's named Jesús to be particularly saintly?"

"I've only known one back at the diner I worked at in St. Paul," I said. "And he definitely wasn't saintly. Fun to work with, though."

"Well, there you go," Loke said. "Let's say that's what I aspire to. Not like my namesake, but still fun."

"I get the sense my grandmother doesn't really like you," I said.

"She doesn't approve of me moving between the worlds all the time," he said with that careless shrug I was starting to think of as sort of his trademark. More with the right shoulder than the left, but with minimal tensing of muscles because the mood this shrug was meant to convey wasn't worth all that much effort.

"She told me lots of people go down to Runde," I said. "She didn't seem bothered by it."

"Well, it's not *lots* of people. It's just a few," he said. "And it's just as you said it: down to Runde. Going beyond that, up to the highway and all that that suggests, that's pretty much just me."

I narrowed my eyes at him. "Thorbjorn was up there. I saw him last night. And you knew what I was talking about when I said it. You knew I wasn't crazy."

"Yes, isn't that interesting?" he said, grinning as he leaned in towards me with a conspiratorial look to his eye. "Why was Thorbjorn there? He *never* goes that far from home."

"He was protecting Lisa," I said, and he looked at me like he found that answer very disappointing. "Lisa. That's why we're here. My grandmother was going to talk to the council about it. Do you know where I'm meant to be?"

He gave me that slow smile again, like he found that question unspeakably suggestive. But then just snapped out of it to point off to our left. "That way. I'll walk with you."

"Thanks," I said.

"So I guess you passed the test?" he said as we walked up another home-lined cobblestoned street.

"I didn't even know there was going to be one, and I don't understand what I did, but I guess the answer to your question is yes," I said. "Do you know anything about it?"

He shook his head sadly. "I don't have an in with that club."

"What club?"

"The council and their hangers-on," he said. "Your grandmother for one. Thorbjorn and his brothers for a bunch of others. But I'm not really a joiner anyway."

"Maybe I'll understand it on my own when I have all my memories back," I said.

"Is that what they told you?" he asked.

I shrugged, but not the way he did it. More of an I don't know than an I don't care.

"Look, you're a bit of a test case. No one who's left has ever come back. Your mother didn't. And then there's the question of whether you even belong here given that you weren't born here."

"That's harsh," I said.

"I'm just talking about how the magic works," he said. "It protects this place, but the spells were cast more than a thousand years ago. I don't think even your grandmother really knows how they work."

"My grandmother is magic," I said. I felt like I was trying that sentence out, seeing if I thought it was true when I said it out loud. But he just shrugged again. "Let me guess; you can't tell me. Or won't, because I'll just know when my memory is back," I said.

He laughed. "I wouldn't keep holding onto that as some big thing," he said. "I mean, you were, what, seven when you were here last?"

"Eight," I said.

"Exactly. So what you remember is going to be just what you knew and understood when you were eight," he said. "You'll remember the children's version of our history."

"What's the children's version?" I said. "Can you give me a summary?"

"Okay, but you're going to have to sit down for this," he said, grabbing my arm and steering me to a bench that sat beside someone's garden gate. He settled me down on the bench then stood back a bit, his hands raised like a conductor about to start a symphony.

"Am I going to regret asking you this?" I asked.

"No. Hush," he said, annoyed that I had interrupted him before he'd even got going. But the smile came right back, his eyes flashing as he started his story. "Close your eyes and picture it: an island nestled in a fjord halfway up the coast of what was once called the North Way."

"Norway," I whispered. "Is this island Runde?"

"No, and stop interrupting," he said, then stepped forward to put a hand over my eyes to keep them closed. "Now picture it. Runde was a fishing village in the 1800s, but this is much longer ago than that, so get that out of your head. No, we're imagining a place that existed in what they call the Viking Age. Harald Fairhair had just become king, the first king of a place called Norway. But we Northmen are an ornery, independent lot. Lots of our ancestors went west to take their chances in the kingless parts of the world."

"Like here?" I asked.

"Shush, chatty one," he said. "Our story is a bit different. You see, the men of our ancestral home were Vikings, true Vikings who sailed out every summer to pillage and raid and come home with their loot before the winter winds started to blow. Every year they did this, but one fateful year the man whom they called chieftain was betrayed. He and his sons were all murdered, by his own brothers. Their bodies were left on that foreign soil, and the murderers set sail for their home, intent on taking the dead chieftain's lands as well as his wealth."

"Yikes," I said.

"But the chieftain's wife Torfa was a witch," Loke said, too caught up in his story now to notice me. "Torfa knew the minute they killed her man and their sons. She knew they were coming. And she knew that the people she had left with her in their ancestral village were no match for the warriors who were on their way.

"By the first light of the next dawn, she commanded her people to pack up everything they could carry and to load it onto the one boat they had left. This wasn't a proper Viking ship, built to cross the seas. It was only built to cross the fjord to allow the people of the island to trade with their neighbors on the mainland. But Torfa was a cunning witch. With her magic, there was room enough on that little boat for every man, woman, and child left in the village from the oldest toothless crone to the babe born just the day before. She told them all they would found a new village on the coast of faraway Iceland, and working together, they would create a new home, a farm richer than any on the island they were leaving behind.

"They pushed out to sea in that ship not built for the sea, but they were too slow. The island was still on the horizon behind them when their own Viking ships came around the bend in the coast, the warriors on board rowing with the strength of men in their prime.

But they weren't heading for the island. They were chasing Torfa and her people.

"Torfa's people rowed as well as they could, but it was never enough. The Viking ships were drawing ever closer, and soon everyone was too tired to row any further. All seemed lost, but Torfa was never one to give up. She summoned every bit of magic she had within herself and performed one last spell: a spell to take them to a safe place, far from the reach of any Viking."

Loke took his hand off my eyes and stepped back. I opened my eyes, blinking in the bright sunlight. "She brought them here?" I guessed.

"She was aiming for Iceland," he said. "She overshot. But she kept her people safe. One moment they were in the North Sea, ships hot on their heels. The next, they were in the middle of Lake Superior. Safe from any Viking; it would be centuries before any kind of ship could navigate this far from the ocean. A lot of canals and locks and such had to be built first."

"Birchbark canoes?" I said.

"Torfa's people soon learned about those," he said. "When they settled here, the Ojibwe were their neighbors. But no one back in the old world knew about those until centuries later."

"Torfa," I said. "I'm named for her, then?"

"Technically, you're Ingrid Torfudottir," he said. "Usually we use our father's names, but the line of daughters of Torfa are all Torfudottir no matter who their fathers are. Of course, that's just you and Nora now. You're the last remaining Torfudottirs."

I sat with this information for a moment, and Loke turned to sit on the bench beside me. Then I glanced over at him. "If they were fleeing other Vikings and reached here, why is this still protected by spells? What are we hiding from?"

"Hey," he said with a smile, "you asked me to sum up the *children's* version. But that's enough for now. We better find Nora before she finds us."

"So there are layers to the magic," I said as we walked. "Villmark is safest, Runde is still pretty safe, and then there's the rest of the world?"

"So they tell us," he said with that little shrug again. "I think I mentioned I was skeptical. Like your cat, I prefer to go where I choose."

"My cat?" I said. It felt like a non-sequitur, but then Loke pointed at the fence around the garden of a house just to our right.

Sure enough, Mjolner was there, bathing his sleek black fur with one of his over-sized paws, paying no attention to me whatsoever.

"Mjolner!" I said and ran over to scoop him up off the fence post. "How did you get out of mormor's house?"

"Speaking of mormor," Loke said, nudging me. I turned to see my grandmother marching towards us looking deeply annoyed. Thorbjorn was trailing behind her. Relief washed over his face when he saw me there.

"Well, that wasn't helpful," my grandmother said to me. "I go to present you to the council, and you're not even there."

"We were catching up," Loke said but fell silent at a glare from my grandmother.

"I have a question," I said as I snuggled against Mjolner's neck. "Where did my cat come from?"

"I assume he sneaked out of my house," my grandmother said with a frown.

"No, I mean originally," I said. "He turned up at my house in St. Paul months ago and refused to leave until I took him in. I tried to turn him in to the pet adoption agency a bunch of times, but he just kept coming back to me. And he can walk through walls, and I think even predict the future, so clearly he's not a normal cat."

"Shows what you know about cats," my grandmother said, scratching Mjolner around his ears. Then she saw me staring at her and blinked in surprise. "Well, I didn't send him."

"But he is *from* here, right?" I asked.

"We have cats here, but none that look like him," Thorbjorn said, touching one of Mjolner's paws. "Does he have six toes?"

"That's not that unusual," I said. "Not like teleporting and the rest. Seriously, none of you know anything about this?"

Thorbjorn shook his head, as did my grandmother. Loke just made that effortless shrug of his. I turned Mjolner around in my arms to look him in the eyes.

"Did you come from here all on your own, Mjolner?" I asked him. "Or are you from some other place? Are you here to protect me or spy on me or what?"

But he just blinked at me, a slow lowering and raising of his eyelids.

In that moment, I would freely believe that he was a talking cat who was just choosing not to speak.

CHAPTER 11

I had to half-jog to keep up with my grandmother, who I was learning was a bit of a fast walker. Mjolner made a little sound of protest in my arms but didn't try to squirm away.

"Did they tell you who Lisa was seeing here?" I asked when I had reached her side.

"You could've just asked me that," Loke said from where he was trailing along behind us, hands in his pockets. "Saved yourself a trip to the council. Not that *that* isn't always fun."

"Hush, you," Thorbjorn said from where he was walking beside him. "We went to the council first as a courtesy."

"And how did that work out for you?" Loke asked. Thorbjorn said nothing, but his stony silence was answer enough.

"Did you?" I asked my grandmother again.

"Yes, actually," my grandmother said. "It wasn't who I was expecting."

"You were expecting it was me, weren't you?" Loke asked, and I could hear the grin all over his voice. "Come on, admit it."

"You are down there more than the rest of us combined," Thorbjorn said to him when my grandmother refused to answer.

"That you know of," Loke said.

"Here we are," my grandmother said, stopping in front of a narrow but long building. We were looking at the north-facing side, so the windows were too small for me to peer through.

"I told you it was Roarr Egilsen," Loke said.

"No, you didn't," Thorbjorn said.

"I implied it," he said. I couldn't help laughing at the annoyance on Thorbjorn's face but clapped a hand over my mouth at the look of betrayal Thorbjorn shot me.

"Sorry," I said.

Loke was rolling back on his heels, hands still in his pockets, and the look on his face as he opened his mouth to speak I just knew meant trouble. But then the garden door swung open, and a young woman stepped out. She jumped when she saw us all lingering there. Her long blond hair was pulled back into a bun so loose most of her hair was still dancing in the breeze all around her face, and she had to reach a hand up to untangle it from her lashes. The blue of her dress was a perfect match for her eyes, but the apron she wore over it was clearly functional, the pockets stuffed and with food stains dotting it here and there.

At first, she said something in Norwegian, but then my grandmother said something else, and the woman looked at me.

"Oh, pardon!" she said. "I didn't realize you were here already, Ingrid Torffudottir. I'm Sigvin." She stepped towards me with her hand outstretched, and I took it. She spoke more like Thorbjorn with a singsong accent, and I realized for the first time that Loke had not. He didn't even really sound like a local from Runde. He spoke like a city-dweller. Just how far had he been straying from home?

Sigvin turned her attention back to my grandmother but continued in her lilting English. "I was just paying my respects. I brought a loaf of my honey rye bread, although I don't suppose that helps much."

"It was a kind gesture, Sigvin," my grandmother said.

"I hope you find-" Sigvin started to say but saw Loke standing there and completely lost her train of thought as her cheeks flushed bright pink. "Oh, hello, Loke."

"Sigvin," he said. "I was just leaving."

"Were you?" my grandmother said, arching one eyebrow.

"Of course. It's going to be all crying and tearing out of hair in there, and that's not my kind of thing," he said. Then he winked at me. "See you, Ingy."

"Ugh, never call me that again," I said.

His grin told me I was going to be hearing that nickname a lot, and I regretted not just holding my tongue. Then he turned and sprinted back up the road, making a right turn at the village square then disappearing from view.

"Why does he always do that?" Sigvin sighed. "He's one way when it's just the two of us and another way when there are other people around."

"Sounds to me like a good reason for it never to be just the two of you," Thorbjorn grumbled. "I need to excuse myself as well. There are a few people I want to talk to and some things I want to look at before it gets dark."

"Yes, of course," my grandmother said. "Love in its purest form and love in its most selfish form, right?"

"It's not much to go on," Thorbjorn said, shaking his head sadly. Then he looked at Sigvin. "Sigvin, may I escort you home?"

Sigvin, who had been looking like she was willing herself not to cry in the middle of the street, immediately perked up. "Yes, that would be lovely."

I turned to my grandmother the moment they were out of earshot. "Why were you repeating what I said about love like it meant something?"

"Because it did," she said. "Of course, when you have a bit more practice, you'll be able to tell us what you actually mean. In the meantime, it's better than nothing to go on."

"Actually, it sounds to me a lot like nothing to go on," I said.

"Let's go inside," my grandmother said. "Perhaps things will be clearer after we talk to Roarr."

I set Mjolner down on the cobblestones and followed my grandmother through the open gate. Everything beyond the garden gate was paved, and there were large containers set out, but the plants within were whithered like the meadow flowers had been. It looked like it would be a cheery space in the summertime. There was even a brick fire pit in one corner, a metal grill resting over the remains of some forgotten fire. Did they eat hamburgers here in Villmark? Or kebabs? Potato salad?

"Ingrid," my grandmother called as she stood waiting for me at the door to the house.

"Sorry," I said. "This is all so modern."

"The village was founded in the early 900s, but time kept moving from there," she told me, then pointed at my shoes to remind me to take them off. They were no longer even remotely white, not after that climb up and around the waterfall. "Our ancestors here in Villmark always had contact with the people around them. They got on very well with the Ojibwe. There was even talk of dissolving the whole village when the Norwegians arrived in the 1800s, of just intermarrying and carrying on as any other immigrants."

"But they didn't?" I said.

"No, they chose to preserve their own memories and culture," she said. "Although it did mark a shift in their language. What came before was something between Norwegian and Icelandic, but after the immigrants came, it shifted closer to Norwegian, although there are still differences. It's a long story. There's a lot I have yet to tell you about Torfa, our founder."

"She was a witch," I said, and when my grandmother's eyebrows went up, I added, "Loke told me."

"Oh, wonderful," she said. It took me a moment to grasp that she was being sarcastic. "Now you have things to unlearn before you learn."

She led the way out of the house's mudroom up to the living space, which was arranged as one great room to make the most of the southerly windows. I could see rows of hills all topped with trees in full autumn glory. It was no lake view, but it was gorgeous in its own way.

"Egil, Ragna," my grandmother said as she crossed the room with her hands extended. They were sitting together on something between a padded bench and a sectional sofa that faced the windows. They murmured their hellos, but I looked past them to the young man tucked in the very corner of that flat sofa, back against the wall and knees drawn up close to his chin.

He had a haunted look to his eyes as he stared without seeing at his own toes. He didn't look up when we came in or even when my grandmother rested a hand on his shoulder to speak close to his ear. He just kept staring, as if he had gotten stuck between two thoughts and couldn't get going again.

"He's taking it hard," Ragna said. "We told him again and again not to get his hopes up, but here we are."

"Well, Ragna, this is scarcely what you were afraid might happen," my grandmother said, sitting down on the bench beside Roarr and putting a hand on one of his socked feet. He didn't react to her touch at all.

"No, you're right," she said. "Murder, they're saying."

"Yes, there's no question about that," my grandmother said. "Did you meet the girl?"

"Oh, of course," Ragna said. "She's been coming to the village since they were both, what, fifteen?" She looked at Roarr like he might suddenly snap out of it and answer her question, but he didn't stir. "Yes, nearly seven years now."

"Never meant to be," Egil said. He was standing and staring out the window at the hills, and I started to get an inkling of where Roarr got his tendency to catatonia from. "Never meant to be. We told him, but he wouldn't hear it."

"Well, I know you both know I don't agree with that assessment," my grandmother said.

"No, of course not," Ragna said, her cheeks flaming as she went to her dining room table in the desperate hunt for something to tidy up. She glanced at me but then quickly looked away again.

"Ragna, I think Ingrid might be getting a bit hungry," my grandmother said, but her eyes were on Roarr. "Perhaps you and Egil can take her to the kitchen and make her a little something. Ingrid, Egil smokes the best fish in Villmark. Be sure he lets you try some."

"Okay," I said. I still had half of the sandwiches she had given me at the Sorensens' place wrapped in the napkin in my pocket, but I could see she wasn't so much concerned about my food intake as she was looking for a moment alone with Roarr.

If only there were a way to chase out the disapproving parents and let me stay. I really wanted to know what Roarr had to say. But I could see that Egil was going to need a little coaxing to come out of his spell.

"What sort of fish do you smoke? Salmon?" I asked.

He looked down at me like I'd just spoken to him in some alien language, but then the words sank in. "Mostly trout, but sometimes coho salmon. I'll get you a little of each."

"Oh dear," Ragna said, looking at a loaf of bread she had picked up from the dining room table. "Sigvin's honey rye isn't going to work with fish. It's better with jam."

"I can try both," I said.

I was going to have to chew very slowly if I was going to avoid having my stomach explode while running interference for my grandmother.

Egil and Ragna took me up a short staircase to the kitchen. It stood over the mudroom and overlooked the great room, and we could still see Roarr staring at his toes as my grandmother spoke to him. I perched on a stool at the kitchen's center island and watched as Egil made two open-faced sandwiches of smoked fish on rye crackers with a dollop of something creamy and a sprig of fresh dill. Ragna added two thin slices of the honey rye bread, one spread with blackberry jam and the other with dark honey.

I ate every bit of it as slowly as I could manage. Ragna moved around the kitchen, wiping down surfaces that were already perfectly clean while Egil went back into his fugue state of standing and staring out the window. I tried starting light conversation now and again, but it was acutely uncomfortable to have every word I say met with complete silence. At least the food was good.

Ragna completed a full circle of cleaning before flinging her cloth down and turning to face me.

"I'm sorry for what we said before," she said.

"What part?" I asked, catching a drip of honey on my tongue just before it splashed down on her clean counter. I moved my hand holding the remaining bit of bread until it was safely over the plate.

"Well, all of it," she said. "I didn't mean any offense."

"Why would I be offended?" I asked.

"Well, because of your parents," she said, blinking in surprise. "But, you know, they were the exception that proved the rule."

"I guess that's why my grandmother feels the way she does," I said, not a hundred percent sure I knew what we were talking about.

"Exactly," Ragna said, clapping her hands together like a pleased child. "She let her own daughter go. That was her choice. If we don't want our son to leave us, that doesn't mean we're judging her in any way, right? We just don't want to lose our only boy."

"Sure," I said. "So, he was planning to move to Runde?"

"Duluth," Ragna said, pronouncing it carefully as if it were some long foreign name with too many consonants. She slid onto one of the other stools and fiddled with the spoon she had used for the jam. "I didn't want my boy to go, but I didn't want it to end this way either."

"Of course not," I said.

"We liked Lisa," she said. "She was a good girl. If they had planned to marry and settle up here, we would've been ecstatic."

"She brought me the salmon," Egil said out of nowhere, still gazing out the window. "We don't get it in the Konallelva, but she used to bring us some every time she came to visit."

Clearly, they both were dealing with a lot of complicated emotions, and I wasn't the one that could help them through any of it. I was too new to this world and its rules and expectations.

"We're going to find out who did this," I promised them both. "Roarr will have justice if not peace."

"Thank you," Ragna said, but automatically, as if she were only telling me what she thought I wanted to hear.

"Ingrid," my grandmother called from the bottom of the stairs. "Time for us to go."

"Thank you for the food," I said. When I came down the stairs, I saw Roarr still sitting exactly as he'd been when I'd gone up to the kitchen. Had he told my grandmother anything useful or had she simply run out of time? She did seem to always feel that however much she had of that, it was never enough. Even now, she was practically pawing the ground in her need to hurry on to the next thing.

I looked back at Roarr one last time before following my grandmother into the mudroom to retrieve our shoes. He didn't look back up at me.

"Is he going to be all right?" I asked her in a whisper as I pulled on my sneakers.

"I don't know," she said with a sigh.

"Did he tell you anything at all?"

"No," she said. "Maybe Thorbjorn will find out something, but it's getting late. I have to get down to the meeting hall before the dinner rush starts."

"Seriously?" I asked. She gave me a quizzical look. "I'm sorry, but everyone up here and down there treats you like your lord of the estate or something, but you're worried about your job as a server?"

"It's all connected," she told me as she tied her last boot and picked up her walking stick. "Ready?"

We walked out of the house and out onto the cobblestone road, and I saw Mjolner was still there, washing his ears while he waited for us. My grandmother started that fast walk of hers back towards the waterfall, but I just stood there looking at Mjolner.

"Mormor?" I said, and she turned back, not trying to hide her impatience. "Can I stay up here for a bit? Wander around?"

She frowned, and I was just wondering what I, a grown woman, was going to do if she told me no. But in the end, she just said, "find Thorbjorn or - ugh! - Loke when you're ready to come home. Don't try to walk down on your own. Promise me."

"I promise," I said. I watched her walk away until she turned the corner and vanished from sight. Then I turned to Mjolner. "Okay, clearly, you were telling me to stay just now. Do you have something to show me?"

He looked at me for a long moment and then just resumed washing his ears.

CHAPTER 12

I was still standing there, staring dumbfoundedly at my cat when I felt someone watching me. I looked up to see Loke leaning on a fence a few houses down. Grinning, of course.

"Something amuses you?" I asked, crossing my arms.

"I like your cat," he said. "He keeps his own secrets, doesn't he?"

I couldn't argue with that, but at the moment, it was a less than helpful trait. I left him to his bathing and went to stand closer to Loke.

"Are you going to call on Roarr?" I asked.

"Wasn't planning on it," he said.

"He's pretty shaken up," I said. "You knew he was seeing Lisa?"

"I knew they were into each other before they even did, and they've been a thing since we were all kids," he said. "His parents didn't approve, but as they got older, that became less of an obstacle in their minds."

"Was it a healthy relationship?" I asked.

Loke looked appalled at the question. "Who am I to judge a thing like that? I have no idea what they were like when it was just the two of them. And most of the time they spent together, it was just the two of them."

"But he was happy before?" I.persisted.

"I don't know. He was just Roarr," Loke said. "He didn't talk about stuff like that."

"You can't tell if someone is happy or not if they don't tell you?"

"Usually not even when they do," Loke said. "People lie, you know. Some people lie a lot."

"That's a dark view," I said. He just shrugged that careless shrug of his. "Okay, Mr. Dark View, was there a third point in a love triangle with the two of them? Someone here or in Runde or maybe where Lisa went to school?"

'Well, anything's possible," he said.

"You know, for someone who claims to know things, you're not particularly helpful," I said.

"Maybe you're asking the wrong questions," he said.

I felt like he wanted me to ask him something specific, but he wasn't going to give me any hints. He just stood there grinning at me and waiting for me to figure it out.

Clearly, Loke didn't pay enough attention to people's feelings and mental states to give me anything to work on in the motive column.

"Did you see Lisa yesterday at all?" I asked.

"You know, I did," he said, leaning in as if sharing very juicy gossip.

"Who was she with? What did she do?" I asked.

"Well, it's not like I was following her around," he said. "I just saw her passing through the marketplace. So I guess she was shopping. This was at about midday."

"That's it?" I asked. "That's all you know?"

He shrugged again, and I knew that whatever he was dying to tell me, it hadn't been that. I sighed and looked around for inspiration. My eyes landed on a potted plant sitting by someone's garden gate. It still had a few green leaves on it, but I had no idea what sort of plant it was. It got me thinking all the same.

"Lisa was poisoned," I said, and that slow grin started spreading over Loke's face again. "The police are still working on just what sort of poison it was, but do you know of anyone here that has access to anything like that? Do you have an apothecary or something?"

He was grinning so wildly I thought he might be about to explode with glee. Clearly, that had been the right question. "Follow me," he said. I looked back toward Roarr's house, but Mjolner had disappeared.

I followed Loke.

We went back to the village square and then took the road that led to the south end of the village. It ended in a fenced-in garden that wasn't attached to any house. The opening was an arched trellis hung with now-dry vines, and there was no gate. The space within was laid out in raised beds of well-spaced plants, each with a wooden stake labeled with its name in runes. Paving stone paths wound through the raised beds, dividing and converging in a knotwork pattern that I was sure was quite lovely if seen from above. At the far end of the garden stood an immense greenhouse stuffed full of green growing things.

"What's this?" I asked.

"The village gardens," he said. "We grow our own vegetables, herbs, spices, and medicinal things. A lot of people have variations in their private gardens, but an example of everything is also kept here like a public trust."

"There are poisons here," I said.

"Many," he said. "Some your police force will have ruled out already. There are also other, rarer things that will take them longer to isolate if that's what was used."

"And the entire village has access to this?" I asked.

"The entire village," he agreed.

"You know, the thing I was trying to accomplish was narrowing down the list of suspects," I sighed.

"Good luck with that," he said. "Everyone here had means, motive, and opportunity."

"Everyone had *motive*?" I said. "Everyone I've spoken to has had nothing but good things to say about Lisa."

"Of course they do; she just died," he said. "All I'm saying is just about anyone is capable of murder, and they don't necessarily need a good reason."

"You'd make a terrible detective," I said.

The greenhouse door opened, and two women about my age came

out. Clearly sisters, they were both tall, muscled, and tanned. One had light blond hair, and the other had dark blond hair, but aside from that, they could be twins. They saw Loke standing there and scowled at him, but when he waved, they came over.

"You should really meet these two," he whispered to me, and then when they were closer, he said, "Nilda, Kara, this is Ingrid Torfudottir."

"Really?" the light blond one said. "I heard you were in town. It's good to meet you. I'm Nilda Mikkelsen, and this is my sister Kara."

I shook her hand and then Kara's. If I had to guess, I'd say Nilda was older, but not by much.

"Ingrid here is trying to figure out who murdered Lisa," Loke told them.

Kara hissed in a breath. "So it *was* murder, then. I had hoped that was just a rumor."

"Poison," I said. "We don't know what kind yet."

"And Loke brought you here?" Nilda said, shooting Loke a look. "How is that helpful?"

"She wanted to see an apothecary," he said.

"Or something," I added lamely.

"Your first mistake was letting this one take you around," Kara said and made shooing motions with her hands at Loke. "Go on, get. We'll take it from here."

"You know I'll just be back again," he said, but he did leave, stopping to wink at me from the arched gateway. "See you, Ingy."

Then he was gone.

"We knew Lisa," Nilda told me. "She and Roarr used to hang out with a bunch of us when we were teenagers. We used to have bonfires over on the next hill and stay up all night."

"Used to?" Kara teased. "The last one was a week ago."

"I was talking about back then. It's not the same as it used to be," Nilda said. "Beer tastes different when you're not stealing it from your parents, right?"

"I guess so," I said. I had been working pretty much fulltime since I was old enough to get a job and had never had much time for parties. But I was familiar with the concept. "Roarr is taking it hard."

"We know, we went to see him already," Nilda said, looking to Kara, who nodded her agreement. "Poor guy."

"Do you know if there was another guy at all?" I asked. "Maybe here, maybe where Lisa went to school?"

"No," Nilda said, but they were both shaking their heads. "We didn't know Lisa as well as Roarr did, but I just don't see her doing that to him."

"She adored him," Kara said. "Everyone could see that."

"Did you see her at all yesterday?" I asked. "Loke saw her in the village market at about noon, but she didn't die until after nightfall. That's a lot of time to account for."

"I didn't. Did you?" Nilda asked Kara.

"I saw her walking down the road from the meadow," Kara said. "She was just coming out of the woods, but she looked lost in thought. She didn't see me when I waved to her, but I didn't think anything of it at the time."

"From the meadow, like she was just coming up from Runde?" I asked. "So, she was here and left and came back again?"

Kara shrugged. "I wasn't paying a lot of attention. She just seemed, like I said, sort of lost in thought. You know, summer is over. Decision time. Hence the distraction."

"Anyway, I wouldn't put a lot of faith in anything Loke said he saw," Nilda said. "He could be telling you the truth, or he could be bending the truth for some perverse reason of his own."

"Or he could be lying," I said.

Nilda and Kara looked at each other. "Maybe? But I don't think so," Nilda said. "I think outright lying isn't Loke's style."

"Too easy," Kara said. "Why make something up when bending the truth just so requires so much more skill."

"Still, if you want to figure out what happened to Lisa, there's someone you absolutely need to talk to," Nilda said.

"Who's that?" I asked.

"Thorbjorn," they both said at once. I laughed.

"Oh, yeah. We've met. Last night, actually."

"Isn't he just..." Kara trailed off, but the way she was fanning herself conveyed her feelings about his hotness well enough.

"He's just," I agreed. "Single, I take it?"

"Married to the job, more like it," Kara said glumly.

"He's probably investigating this already," Nilda said. "We don't have an official police force like you do down there, but if we did have a sheriff, it would be Thorbjorn."

"And his brothers," Kara said. "They break up fights and keep the peace."

"Nobody tangles with a Thor, not even when they're drunk out of their mind," Nilda said.

"The Thors guard the passage between Villmark and Runde, right?" I said.

"Yes. That's their official duty, and they take it in turns," Nilda said. "They also patrol the hills. But Thorbjorn has more of a sense of mission than the others. He's out in the hills more than he's home, protecting us from what lurks out there."

"What lurks out there?" I asked.

They traded another look, then Kara said, "you know what? We should just take you to his place, and you can ask him yourself."

I nodded, but I knew that wasn't going to happen. Or at least, if I did, I doubted he would answer. It was one of those secrets I was supposed to remember on my own in my own time.

But I got the feeling that whatever lurked out there was something big and dangerous, feral and monstrous. Not the sort of thing that would've poisoned Lisa and left her on the highway. So for the moment, it didn't really matter.

One mystery at a time.

CHAPTER 13

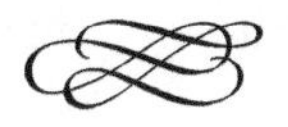

Nilda and Kara led me down the one road I hadn't yet gone down, the one to the north. Not long after we passed the village square, the road started climbing at a steep grade. It was so steep that each house stood above its neighbor to the south, its foundation level with the other's flat roof. I was winded by the time we reached the very last house, but when Nilda and Kara stopped at its garden gate, my feet carried me on to the very end of the road. It ended in another public park with benches sitting among trees arranged in a circle around the turnabout, but what captivated me was the view beyond.

Hill after hill rose up, each higher than the last, all covered in trees. That was familiar enough to me. But beyond those hills were... mountains. I blinked and rubbed my eyes and looked again, but they were still there.

"There aren't any mountains in Minnesota," I said to Nilda and Kara.

"But that's Norway," Nilda said.

"Kinda," Kara amended.

"Kinda," Nilda agreed.

"You mean I can just keep walking past all those hills, and I'd be in Norway?" I asked.

"Don't do that," Nilda said, her face gravely serious.

"No, don't try it," Kara said. "It's not proper Norway. It's a Norway that's not... human-friendly."

"Monsters?" I said.

"Everything," Kara said. "The witch Torfa carved out this place for us using powerful magics. But you can't just create something from nothing, so what she did was make a protective bubble here in Minnesota using magic she pulled from where she had always pulled it from. That other version of her homeland. The dark magical reflection of her Norway."

"If someone went through there, would they end up in modern Norway?" I asked.

"I suppose if there were another witch somewhere who had created another protective bubble, maybe?" Kara said, but Nilda was glaring at her fiercely, so she added, "anyway, don't try it."

"Things come out of there from time to time," Nilda said. "That's why the Thors live here on the edge of town. They spend as much time out there as they do here."

"Especially Thorbjorn," Kara sighed. "You never see that one at a party. Such a shame." Then she waved for me to come back down from the park, and I walked back to join them as they knocked on the front gate. Just a single rap, like my grandmother would do. Nilda was about to open it so we could continue on to the front door when it swung open on its own, and we saw Thorbjorn standing there.

"Hello Nilda, Kara," he said, sounding half-distracted. Then he saw me. "And Ingrid. I was just heading out. But never mind. Would you all like to sit for a minute?"

We followed him into the front garden to a circle of benches gathered around the remains of a bonfire. The flames had died down, and the embers were dark, but the heat was still intense, especially under the light of the afternoon sun. We sat down on the benches, but Thorbjorn still seemed distracted. He stared at the remains of the fire as if he had already forgotten the three of us were there at all.

"He's like this a lot," Nilda whispered close to my ear. "The sweetest guy, but always with the weight of the world on his shoulders. If you can get him to set it aside for a few hours, though, he's the life of the party."

I nodded. But I wondered how she knew this since Kara said he never went to parties.

"Ingrid told us about Lisa," Kara said to Thorbjorn, resting a hand on his knee. "That it was murder, I mean. Do you want to talk about it?"

"I was there," he said, "when she passed."

"I'm so sorry," Kara said, then waited for him to go on. At first, he just continued staring at the embers, but then he sat back on his bench as if deliberately pulling himself out of his melancholy.

"I was walking the hills, as I often do," he said. "Just north of here. I was following a trail of tracks I thought might be from a bear, but I wanted to be sure it really was just a black bear and not something more. Just an ordinary evening, in other words. But I had a sudden feeling that something had been torn asunder."

"Thorbjorn has a bond with the magic that protects the village," Nilda whispered to me. "His people didn't create it, but they've always protected it."

"I can feel when something has crossed that barrier that shouldn't," Thorbjorn said, and Nilda flushed a little as she realized her whispering hadn't been as quiet as she thought.

"Do you know what it was?" I asked.

Thorbjorn shook his head. "Animals cross it all the time, like the bear I was tracking. And people cross it, more than they're supposed to. But this was different. This was pure malevolence. Raw anger. And it hadn't crossed at the falls. I followed that feeling of wrongness down the hill. There is a secret path that runs that way that only my family knows of. I followed it all of the way down past the restaurant and out onto the highway. The fog was so thick I couldn't see anything, but I felt the moment that malevolence just slipped away."

"What do you mean?" I asked. "It disappeared?"

He frowned even more deeply as he thought it over. "No, it was like the anger dissipated. The power went out of it, and then it just slinked away. Without the fog, I might have seen it. Or maybe not, who knows?"

"But you found Lisa," Kara said.

"Yes. She was lying in the middle of the highway, and I ran out to her. I took her hand and felt her life slipping away. Then I heard a car approaching. I knew I didn't have time to pick her up and carry her out of the way, so I did what I could. I stopped the car." He cleared his throat and shot me a nervous look. "Sorry about that."

"Not your fault," I said. "Believe me; no one is happier that I hit that tree rather than run her over than I am. Even if she was dead before I got there."

"Was she dead when you got there?" Kara asked Thorbjorn.

"No," he said, and the weight on his shoulders must have doubled because we all saw him bow down beneath it. "I was there with her for her last breath."

"I'm glad you were," Kara said. "I'm glad she wasn't alone."

"Me too," Nilda said. "She didn't deserve what happened to her, but I'm glad you were there with her in the end."

Thorbjorn just nodded. I thought he was going to slip back into his melancholy, but instead he looked up at me. "That's why the runes I cast for you to read had such power. Because in her last breath, she put a debt on me. I have to find her killer and bring them to justice. And I think you are bound by it as well."

"Me?" I asked.

"Your reading," he said. "Didn't it feel to you like something else was moving through you when you read what you saw?"

I didn't say anything. None of the answers that came to me were going to be of any comfort to him. I mean, I was still half-convinced I had just been making things up. I certainly didn't feel like some greater power had worked through me.

Although, what would that feel like?

"Have you seen anything more? Since we parted?" he asked eagerly.

"Sorry, no," I said. He nodded, but I could tell he was disappointed. "I've been trying to figure out if Lisa was seeing someone else," I said.

"Lisa?" he said.

"Well, what I saw, it was all about two forces with something or someone caught in the middle, right? I said. "So if Lisa were caught in the middle of something, I would guess that one side was Roarr. But I haven't had any luck finding the other side."

"Lisa," he said again, but then shook his head. "No, that's wrong."

"Well," I said, and I could feel my cheeks flushing. I wanted to say that I had never claimed to have any rune-reading powers, so it could hardly be surprising when I failed at the task, but I bit my tongue instead.

"No, not Lisa," Thorbjorn said. "That's not what I got out of your words. No, the one caught in the middle is Roarr. Isn't that what you meant?"

I bit my tongue again. There was nothing to be gained by pointing out that I hadn't even met Roarr when I had said those things, and Lisa had been dead before I drove into town. I hadn't meant *anything* by what I'd said.

And yet, what he said felt right when I let it sink in. "If anyone looks like they're caught in a maelstrom, torn apart by two opposing forces, it's Roarr," I said.

Kara nodded her agreement. "Torn apart. That's him right now."

"So Lisa was his purest of loves, right? So what was his most selfish of loves?" I really wished I had bit my tongue for a third time before letting the next words slipped out, but I didn't. "His mother?"

"No, no, no," all three of them said, shaking their heads and shifting uncomfortably on their benches.

"Not his mother, no," Thorbjorn said. "But I think you're on the right track."

"Of course you do, you were already thinking it," I said.

"Yes, well." He cleared his throat uncomfortably.

"What are you going to do now?" Kara asked him.

"Whatever it is, we want to help," Nilda added.

Thorbjorn looked up at the sky. "I want to retrace my steps from last night before it gets dark," he said. "I have a few hours yet."

"You think you'll feel that thing again?" Kara asked.

"Probably not," he allowed. "But I want Ingrid to come with me. She might see something I miss."

"Me?" I said. "I doubt it. But sure, I'll come."

"Good," he said, slapping his thighs and then rubbing his hands together.

"And us?" Nilda asked.

"Kara, I want you to go to Roarr's house," he said. "Keep an eye on the family. Make sure they're doing okay, but also watch out for any suspicious characters that might come by or lurk around the place."

"I can do that," she agreed.

"Nilda, I want you to do the same at Lisa's parents' house," he said. "They know you in Runde?"

"A bit," she said. "They know I'm Lisa's friend, even if they don't know me well."

"Good," he said. "And see if you can find out what poison their police suspect was used. I imagine when anyone knows, they'll tell her parents first."

"I'm on it," Nilda said.

We went to the garden gate and parted ways, Kara and Nilda heading together to the village square before breaking off in different directions. I looked up at Thorbjorn. "Where to now?"

"This way," he said, pointing out to the hills.

"Where you told me earlier not to go?" I asked.

"Where I told you not to go *alone*," he amended. "But you'll be with me."

"Fully armed?" I said, looking around for his weapons. He wasn't wearing them.

"Actually, I need to get changed before we go down there," he said. It was a little hard to tell through the beard, but I think he was blushing. "I'm not supposed to be in Runde dressed like this."

"Oh. Right," I said.

"I'll still have a knife on me. You'll be perfectly safe," he promised.

"I'm not worried," I assured him. He looked like he could wrestle a bear into submission if he had to.

He was backing up towards his house when something behind me caught his eye. I turned to see Mjolner sitting in the middle of the road, once again calming washing his ears.

"He didn't have to wait out here. Why didn't you bring him into my family's garden with you?" Thorbjorn asked.

"He wasn't with me at the time," I said. "He comes and goes as he likes."

Mjolner gave his left ear one more swipe and then got up and walked away, back toward the center of town.

"You know, I think we should follow him," I said.

"Then that's what we'll do," Thorbjorn said, and came back out into the road, shutting his gate behind him with a click.

I had expected to have to argue a bit more for my "let's follow the cat" plan, but apparently, that wasn't as weird a plan as I thought it was.

This town was definitely going to take a little getting used to.

CHAPTER 14

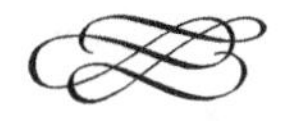

Mjolner led us past the well to the road to the southern part of town.

"I was just down here," I said to Thorbjorn.

"Were you?"

"Loke was showing me the gardens," I said. "Mjolner wasn't with us, or I guess he could've shown me whatever he wanted me to see then."

"To you and Loke?" he asked. There was something strange about his tone. Like he was trying too hard to sound like this was only a casual interest.

"What does that mean?" I asked.

"You've been spending a lot of time with Loke, that's all I'm saying," he said.

"I think it's more like he's been spending a lot of time with me," I said. "And in the end, he wasn't much help."

"Wasn't he?" Thorbjorn asked. He sounded as gravely serious as ever, but I was pretty sure he was amused by that.

"I mean, he was acting like he knew all about everything since he knew about Roarr and Lisa, but when I asked more questions, he had nothing. And then he acted like he knew just what poison was used to kill her, but he just brought me to the garden at the end of this road and announced that it was full of things that could be used as poisons and that everyone in town could get them anytime they wanted."

"Hmm," Thorbjorn said noncomittally.

"Does that mean you think he's right?" I asked.

"No," Thorbjorn said. "Granted, we don't know what poison was used yet, but I think we can guess that it was a rather subtle one or the police down there would already know what they're looking for."

"Loke said some of these plants were rare," I said. "Do they come from the old world?" I pointed a thumb back over my shoulder, although the distant mountains were completely hidden from view this far south.

He raised his eyebrows in surprise. "You acquire information at astounding speed, Ingrid Torfudottir."

"People like to tell me things," I said. "But am I right?"

"Yes, you are correct," he said. "But Loke is wrong about everyone in the village being an equally likely suspect. The dangerous plants are sequestered in one corner of the greenhouse, and they are protected by certain spells. Only their guardian can handle them."

"And who's their guardian?" I asked.

Thorbjorn came to an abrupt halt, and I realized that Mjolner had stopped to bathe again. He had just plopped down on the road between two houses, or so I thought at first. Then I noticed the little path that squeezed between the two houses' fences.

"She lives just down there," Thorbjorn said, pointing down the path. "She'd know if anything was missing. You know, I wasn't sure if this was going to be worth the walk, but I'm starting to think your cat is really on to something."

"Really?" I said. He had seemed pretty confident when he said we should follow the cat. Had that been for my benefit, because it was my idea?

"I should tell you, the guardian of the plants is Halldis," he said. "You remember her from before?"

"How could I forget her?" I asked. "Is she likely to hit me with her whammy again?"

"I would say no because I'll be there with you, but then I saw her do it just this morning with your grandmother right there, so all bets are off."

I looked down the path. I could just see a little hut at the end of it, rounded with a great big round door like a hobbit would live in. "Why does she live so far off the road?"

"Who knows?" he shrugged. "She's a bit of a recluse. But she knows more about those plants than anyone else in the village. Except possibly your grandmother. We should definitely talk to her. Especially considering..." he gestured to Mjolner, who had sprawled out to take a nap in the afternoon sun.

"After you," I said.

Thorbjorn's shoulders barely fit between the two fences. Then the fences ended, and we were in a little garden filled with plants that were thriving despite the lateness of the season. I didn't recognize a single thing. All of the leaves and flowers had strange shapes to them, and even their hue tended to a purplish sort of green. We were in a small artificial gorge, rock walls enclosing the space behind the neighbors' fences, and the breeze didn't stir the air. The smell was thick and noxious, and my head was feeling swimmy like it had after I'd hit my head.

"Is this normal?" I asked, suddenly grateful I was still carrying a walking stick around. I needed it in that moment just to stay upright.

"Let's go inside. I think the air will be clearer there," Thorbjorn said and crossed the garden to knock on that round, red door.

He had to knock three times before it opened, and even then, it opened only wide enough for Halldis to peer out with suspicious eyes. But when she saw it was Thorbjorn standing on her front step, she threw the door wide open.

"Thorbjorn!" She said, leaning against the door she was holding open in a way that made all of her ample curves hit maximum curve. Then she said something in Norwegian that washed right over me.

"If you don't mind, I'd like if we could speak English? Ingrid and I just have a few questions for you, but she doesn't remember our language," he said.

Halldis looked confused in a pretty sort of way that was clearly a practiced response. Then she saw me standing there and scowled when I gave her a little wave. She quickly pulled her face back into a bright smile and aimed it back at Thorbjorn.

“Certainly I can speak English,” she said. Her accent was stronger than Thorbjorn’s, but she spoke so slowly and precisely that I had no trouble understanding her. “But questions? I'm not sure what you could possibly want to ask me about, but I'll help in any way I can," she said. "Would you like some tea?"

"No, thanks," Thorbjorn said as he followed her inside. I also shook my head, but she didn't see it, and I was sure she was planning to pretend I wasn't even there as much as she could.

The inside of her little hut was all one circular room, the roof peaked overhead all but obscured by the bundles of dried herbs hanging from every support beam. At least these plants had a cleaner smell than the ones outside.

I looked around the room in a sweeping circle, starting with the door. Closest to the floormat where we left our shoes, there was a table covered with bowls, mortars, and pestles with curving shelves against the wall next to it holding dozens of jars of various powders and liquids. Then there were a few stacked wooden chests that separated that area from the bed, and another stack of chests between the bed and the table and chairs set against the far wall. The remaining space was padded benches drawn around a low table, which was where Halldis was waving Thorbjorn to sit down. Then she turned to the firepit that dominated the center of the room and pushed a kettle on a metal hook that had been resting off to one side to hang over the center of the fire.

"I was about to have a spot of tea myself, I hope you don't mind," she said as she settled onto the same bench as Thorbjorn, so close she had to tip her head back to look him in the eye.

"Not at all," he said. "We wanted to talk to you about Lisa."

"Lisa?" she frowned, again with the air of a practiced gesture. I suppose it did take some work to craft a facial expression that both conveyed the mood of puzzled confusion without creating any unattractive lines, but she had nailed it.

"Roarr's fiancée," Thorbjorn told her. Then at her continued confusion, he added, "Roarr Egilsen? His fiancée was a Runde girl?"

"Oh!" Halldis said, clapping her hands together. "Yes, I have heard about that. But surely, this is a matter for the Runde police force?"

"There is no Runde police force. Just a county sheriff," I said, but she ignored me.

"They're working on it," Thorbjorn said, "but I have reason to believe that the murderer may be one of us."

"Oh, really?" Halldis said, pressing a hand to her chest as if the thought hurt her heart. "Oh, that's dreadful."

"Thorbjorn said you know more than anyone about poisons," I said. This time I got her attention.

"Oh," she said, blinking several times as she looked at me. I suspected she adored being complimented but wasn't sure if she wanted to take one from me. "Well, I suppose that's true. Still, I'm not sure how I can help. They have her body now, don't they? And without seeing her, I don't know what I can conclude."

"What if you had a toxicology report?" I asked.

"I don't even know what this is," she said with a laugh and got up from the bench to move the whistling kettle off the flame using a fold of her apron as a hot pad.

"They might have a substance name," I said.

"Or some idea of what symptoms she might have had," Thorbjorn added. "If her tongue had a particular color, or if there was a detectable odor."

"I'm not sure their names will be the same as our names," she said. "But the symptoms might help. Still, it seems like the best plan is to let Runde deal with their own troubles."

"But if she was killed here and then moved down there, they will never solve the murder, will they?" I asked.

She made a show of busying herself with making tea. I knew stalling when I saw it, but I didn't press. Only after she'd set the heavy iron kettle back on the hook did she dust off her hands and smooth out her apron then look at me. "Do you have a reason to believe that was the case? That she was moved?"

"Just a hunch," I said.

"Well, you're new," she said. "You don't know how things work here."

"Tell me," I said, "how do things work here?"

"Murder isn't such a big deal," she said with a shrug. "There's a price to be paid from one family to another, sure, but things happen."

"That's not true," I said, then looked to Thorbjorn. "Is that true?"

"Not in this case," he said. "She wasn't one of us. Harming her broke our highest law in Villmark. It risks revealing us to the world."

"But the fact that someone who was breathing yesterday isn't today, that's not a big deal?" I asked.

"That's not what I said," he grumbled.

"She was trying to break up a family," Halldis said. "If killing her was the only way to remove her, so be it."

My mouth opened and closed, then opened again. I gaped at Thorbjorn.

"Right," he said, getting to his feet. "I'm going to see about getting you that list of symptoms, Halldis."

"I will be happy to lend my expertise in any way I can," she said, pouring her steeped tea into a cup. "I do hope I can help. It's not the murder that bothers me so much as the secrecy, though. If it had been me protecting my own son, you would've found me in the middle of the village square standing over her body and showing everyone the bloody knife still in my hands."

"Lovely," I said, but Thorbjorn caught my elbow and propelled me towards the door.

"I'm just being honest, my dear," she said with a very fake smile.

"She's baiting you," Thorbjorn hissed at me, and I bit back what I had been about to say back at her. She followed us to the door and took up that curvy pose again as we went back outside.

"Come again anytime, Thorbjorn," she purred at him. He growled something indecipherable in response. He still had his hand on my elbow and was pulling me towards the gap in the fences almost faster than my feet could keep up. I was tempted to dig my heels in and refuse to go any further, but I was pretty sure in his current mood he'd probably just throw me over his shoulder and carry me out of there.

"Oh, and dear Ingrid," Halldis called from the doorway behind us. "Give a message to your grandmother for me, will you? Tell her she's clearly made a very grave mistake if she thinks you're the one to take up her mantle. She's waited for you for years and years, but you're clearly not the one."

I turned to look back over my shoulder even as Thorbjorn continued to pull me along. There was a look of delicious triumph on Halldis' face as she closed the door.

But her sick burn might've been more effective if I had, say, understood it at all.

CHAPTER 15

"Are we sure she's not evil?" I asked when we were back out on the road, and it felt safe to say such things out loud.

Thorbjorn laughed.

"I'm serious," I said.

"All right," he said, wiping at his eyes. "No, I don't think she's evil. Come on, let's walk back up to my house so I can change."

"What's wrong with what you're wearing?" I asked.

"We're going down to the highway to look for clues," he said. "I can't go down there dressed like this. And I'm sure you can guess why. Your grandmother is never going to forgive me for being seen last night. Lucky for me, I was only seen by you."

I fell into step beside him to yet again cross the entire village, but Mjolner stayed where he was, napping on the warm cobblestones. Crazy cat.

"Evil might be too big of a word," I said, "but she's not trying very hard not to look guilty."

"Her opinions aren't unusual here," Thorbjorn said. "Murder is rare, but when it does happen, it's usually for the sake of ending some long-standing grudge. Halldis isn't wrong about secrecy being worse than the original crime. Owning up to what you did and making amends to the kin involved usually takes care of the matter. Occasionally banishment is the only way to deal with a person who just can't get along with anyone." What I was thinking must have shown on my face because he quickly added, "did I mention it's rare? It's rare. Very rare."

"So you don't think she's guilty because you believe her when she says she'd wait out in public with the murder weapon to confess everything?" I asked.

"No," Thorbjorn said. "She just doesn't fit the rest of the puzzle, does she?"

"I think we should try talking to Roarr again," I said. "He's the most likely person to actually know something."

"I agree, but I don't think he's ready to come out of the state he's withdrawn into," Thorbjorn said.

"What if it isn't just grief making him act that way?" I asked. "What if he saw something? What if he did something?"

"If anyone can bring him out of that state, it's your grandmother," Thorbjorn said. "It means something that she chose not to."

"Did she?" I asked. "She talked to him. I don't think he answered really."

"She could bring him out if she wanted to," Thorbjorn said. "I'm guessing where he's at now, he needs to be there for a while before he can deal with all that's happened. When he's ready, he'll come back out. And if he doesn't, your grandmother will pull him out of it."

"You sound awfully sure," I said.

"I am," he said. We had reached his house again, and he looked up at the sky. "It's going to be dark soon. We have to hurry or else I'd bring you in to meet my family. But if we did that, we'd be stuck here for hours." He sighed. "Wait here; I'll be just an eyeblink."

"Sure," I said. He went in through the gate, and I heard voices greeting him when he disappeared into the snug little house. Four brothers, all his size. How did they fit in that little house?

I wandered up to the top of the hill, but this time I wasn't looking out towards the gray mountains but in towards the lake. I could see all of the village of Villmark spread out before me, and the river as it crossed the meadow. The top of the falls was all spray glowing gold in the setting sun. I couldn't see Runde itself - the angle was all wrong - but I could see the bridge and the highway.

But mostly I could see the lake. Even with the sun sparkling over its surface, it looked cold. It always looked cold. It would be nice if warm, inviting things felt like home to me, but the only thing that felt like part of my world was that steel gray lake. I could almost feel the skeletons of every ship it had sunk to keep within itself forever, down in its cold, dark depths.

"Ready," Thorbjorn said as he emerged from the gate. He was wearing jeans and a faded flannel shirt over a black T-shirt and was just tugging a watchman's cap over his hair. "Do I look like an ordinary person?"

"Sure. Just your ordinary bodybuilder dressed for a trip to the fish market," I said.

"Huh?"

"You're fine," I said. Then he jumped like he had just realized he was forgetting something and ducked back into his house's yard. I heard a clatter of wood, and when he emerged this time, he had a spear in his hands.

"Okay, that's not going to blend," I said.

"I'll hide it," he said. I wanted to see how he pulled off that trick, but my good humor faded when he added, "I'm not walking through these woods with nothing to defend myself but a knife."

"I don't have anything," I said, suddenly feeling anxious.

"You don't need anything. You have me," he said, then pointed down at my sneakers. "And those. Those are your best weapons."

"I think you might be overestimating my running skills," I said. "Especially in this terrain."

"Adrenaline is a powerful motivator," he said. "Come on. We're losing the light."

I followed him past the trees and benches to another meadow of dried grass. Beyond that was another forest of birch and evergreen trees. It didn't look particularly scary when I was still in the grass, but as soon as we were under the canopy, everything became darker, colder, and far too still.

"Why is it so quiet?" I whispered as we walked.

"This is normal," he said, but I noticed he was keeping the spear at the ready.

"This is where I'm not supposed to go, isn't it?" I asked.

"It's where you're not supposed to go *without me*," he said. "Now, let's see. I saw the bear tracks just about... yes, there they are."

I'm glad he didn't consult me. I couldn't see a thing but dry leaves and mossy rocks and ground so muddy that it was going to drive the last nail into my new shoes' coffin. He looked around as if getting his bearings then waved for me to follow him further downhill. It wasn't as steep as the path up to the waterfall, but the ground was much slicker, and I was once again grateful for the walking stick. I could see why my grandmother kept a whole bucket of them by her door.

"There's your tree," Thorbjorn said. I had been looking down at my own feet, carefully placing each of my steps, and hadn't heard any traffic sounds, so I was a bit surprised when I lifted my head to see the highway, not a stone's throw away. And closer still was the shattered remains of the tree I had hit.

"Wow, I had no idea I had hit it so hard," I said. I felt a twinge of guilt. That tree hadn't done anything to deserve this. There was a ribbon tied around its trunk, and I suspected a maintenance crew would be coming by in the next day or two to cut it down lest it fall over the highway in the next strong wind.

"Do you see anything?" he asked me. At first, I thought he was still looking for bear tracks, but then I realized he meant something else.

"I only saw anything before because you'd thrown those wood staves down and stared at me until I started talking," I said. "What do you want me to see here?"

"Anything," he said. "If it's a true sending, it should just jump out at you, shouldn't it?"

"Should it? I don't know anything about this," I said. Then he stepped closer to me to look me straight in the eyes.

"I know you don't remember it all yet, and even when you do, there's still so much for you to learn," he said. "But I know what I saw in that cavern. You have raw power. I'm not the most sensitive to it, I know. But I think Halldis feels it too. That's why she's always attacking you. She knows you have more power than she could ever hope to touch."

"But I don't," I said. "Or at least I don't feel like I do."

"Even if you don't, we're still both connected to Lisa. You do believe that, don't you?"

I swallowed hard. "I want to believe," I said.

He gave a little nod, like if that were all I had to offer him, he'd accept it. "Let's go out to where she was," he said. "Maybe you'll sense something there."

"Please don't get your hopes up," I said. "I think my cat has more magic than I do, and he didn't come down here with us."

"I just want you to try," he said. "Then, if nothing happens, we'll go back up and try talking to Roarr. Okay?"

"Okay," I said. We broke apart, and I picked my way across the highway's drainage ditch, which was filled with things I really didn't want to dwell on. Why did people still think it was okay to throw garbage out of their cars?

I got to the edge of the pavement, but Thorbjorn wasn't there with me. I looked back to see him stashing the spear behind a tree. Then he reached inside his shirt to take something out of an inside pocket. It was only when he'd crossed the drainage ditch to me that I saw what he was holding.

Dried flowers. He must've gathered them when we were crossing the meadow, but I hadn't seen him do it. And yet it looked like he'd carefully chosen the ones he had taken. They were a little more intact, a little more colorful than the others had been.

"Ready?" I asked. He nodded. I looked both ways, but there was no traffic in sight. We stepped out onto the road.

I wasn't sure if I remembered exactly where she had been, besides just a little north of the tree I had run into. But Thorbjorn was making a beeline to a certain stripe on the road, the last one before the cross-road that ran between the restaurant and the garage. He dropped to one knee and touched the pavement, spreading his fingers wide. Then he set the flowers beside his hand.

I felt like I was intruding on a private moment and started to step back, but he reached out a hand to catch mine and hold me there with him. He didn't let go even when I took the half step back to where I had been.

"Do you feel it?" he asked me without looking up.

"Feel what?" I asked. It was hard to be aware of anything besides his hand holding mine, his fingers tangled up in mine.

"We were drawn here," he said. "Lisa brought us here."

"Now?" I asked, and went down on one knee beside him to press my own hand to the stripe on the road. I felt nothing special. I was suddenly struck with the random thought that I had never actually touched a highway before. So that was weird.

"No, last night," he said. "She was dying. She knew she was dying. She only had a few breaths left. But she brought us to her, you and me."

"How could she do that?" I asked.

"I don't know. But she did." Then he looked up at me, and his green eyes stabbed into mine. "Please, can you try to see?"

I looked down at the road, which told me nothing.

Then I looked at the tangle of flowers. I imagined how I would draw them. With these tapered lines, these muted colors, I would want charcoal. I would want to get my whole hand into it, drawing and rubbing and blending.

Imagining drawing it brought out the shapes, the most basic geometric forms that would be the backbone of the composition. And those shapes just started telling me things.

"She isn't here," I said, and Thorbjorn's head bowed. "But you're right. She's in us. She wants us to find out who did this. But not for revenge. She doesn't have that in her heart." I blinked and realized it was because there were tears in my eyes. "She's worried about everyone else. Everyone she left behind. She wants us to make sure that they're all safe."

"We will," he said, and his hand in mine tightened.

"But first we have to get out of the road," I said, standing up to pull him after me, off the road before the car that had been bearing down on us charged by without slowing.

"Now what?" Thorbjorn asked. He released my hand, and I suddenly felt cold and bereft. I hugged my arms around myself and thought of the sweaters that were waiting for me in my car just a few hundred feet away.

"Now Roarr," I said. "That was her strongest thought. We have to talk to Roarr."

"Of course," he nodded, and headed back to where he had stashed his spear.

But my steps were slow as I followed. Because what I felt hadn't been clear at all. Her strongest feelings were fear and Roarr, but was it fear for Roarr, or fear of Roarr?

It was another maelstrom of opposites, and I felt like Thorbjorn and I were the ones in the center of this one, about to be pulled down to the cold depths.

CHAPTER 16

When we reached Roarr's house, Kara stepped out of the shadows and waved us over. "He's not there," she said.

"Where did he go?" Thorbjorn asked.

"Down to Runde," she said. "You don't want to go in there. His parents are flipping out. They didn't see him sneak out."

I looked up at the house, but the windows on this side were small and had blinds drawn down over them. I could see light and shadows, but the shadows were unformed, not even so much as a silhouette to hint at what was moving around inside.

"Why would he go down to Runde?" I asked.

"He's at the meeting hall," Thorbjorn guessed. Kara nodded.

"I followed him down there. He didn't see me; I just wanted to see what he was up to. He went in and ordered a beer and then just sat by himself, nursing it. Maybe he couldn't stand to be home anymore. Not that I blame him. Just in the time I've been watching the place, I swear every unattached young woman in this entire village has been by. His fiancée died less than twenty-four hours ago, the vultures."

"They're just being kind," Thorbjorn said, "paying their respects."

"Paying your respects doesn't usually involve so much preening beforehand," Kara said. Then she turned to me, "we have a shortage of menfolk."

"And Roarr was going to marry outside the village," I said. "Motive?"

"No one I know was holding that against him," Kara said. "Especially if they'd met Lisa. Having him back on the - and I hate to use this word, but - market is clearly everyone's silver lining in this."

"Everyone but Roarr," Thorbjorn said.

"He didn't speak to any of them that I could see," Kara said. "They were left to try to make inroads with his mother. I'm not sure that's going to help any of their causes, but..." she broke off with a shrug.

"We should go down to Runde," I said. The sun was just starting to set, but my legs were absolutely exhausted from all of the climbing up and down the hills and bluffs. I was going to crash the minute my head touched the pillow. I hoped that would be soon.

"I agree," Thorbjorn said. "Kara, come with us. There's nothing more to do here."

"I was hoping you'd say that," she said, stretching her arms wide as if waiting around had given her a crick in her back. "Maybe spying on him will require ordering a beer or two. You know, just for cover."

"We're not going to spy on him," Thorbjorn said. "We just want to talk to him."

"That will definitely require a beer," Kara grinned. "And you're having one too. You know, to blend in."

We walked together across the village. By the time we reached the meadow, the sun was below the horizon, and the air already had a chill to it. Thorbjorn led the way down the stone stair to the cavern below. The bonfire burst into roaring flame the moment he set foot on the cavern floor, and I could hear the stone door rolling open to the second cavern behind the waterfall.

"Does it sense you?" I asked him.

"It senses any of us," Kara said. "Any Villmarker can pass through freely, although there is usually a Thor here standing guard."

"It's my turn," Thorbjorn said. "I've been busy."

"What do you guard against?" I asked. "Are you afraid someone from Runde might come up here and find this place?"

"This is the gate between our two villages, but that's not all it is," he said. "There are other paths down other caves which you don't see because they are sealed."

"These caves are where our ancestors lived when they first came ashore," Kara said. "I don't think they stayed longer than it took to build proper homes, but this place is still special. The fire marks the first hearth, and all of Torfa's spells center around this place."

"At some point, I'm going to properly learn all these things, right?" I asked.

"That's up to your grandmother," Thorbjorn said. "And you, of course."

Then we were behind the waterfall, and the roar of it made further conversation too difficult.

When we came out on the path on the other side, I saw the meeting hall down below. It looked just like it had when I had seen it from above in Villmark, like a Viking longhouse. The windows were bright with the light from roaring fires, and there were torches set out around the patio area in the back.

I wanted to ask the others which was the illusion, the rundown version I saw in Runde or this one? Would I ever see the Runde version again, or had my perceptions been changed permanently? Had it changed because of what I did with the rune staves by the fire, or if I had looked back from here when I had climbed it this morning would I have seen the longhouse?

But we were too close to the waterfall for words, and once we started down the steep path, it took all my concentration to make sure I didn't fall.

And the people of Villmark came down here to drink? Did they sleep it off in the hall and climb back up in the morning?

The sounds of carousing grew louder than the rush of the river, and when we emerged from the undergrowth, I was nearly knocked off my feet by two men tussling at the edge of the sandpit. But they weren't fighting in earnest, just having a bit of fun.

"Easy," Thorbjorn said, catching them by their collars then releasing them where they were less likely to bowl me over. The two men gave him a nod before resuming their wrestling match. A small crowd was cheering them on from the patio, and a few of them called out to Thorbjorn in surprise as we walked by.

Then he opened the back door, and we stepped into the interior of the hall. Gone were the steel support beams and cheap interior walls of smudged, dirty paint. Everything around me was wood now, wood polished to a honey glow that reflected the light from the immense fireplace that dominated the northern wall. Two long wooden tables ran the length of the room, people in twos and threes sharing the shorter benches.

A tall, gray-haired man smiled an apology as he squeezed past me to get out the door, and I recognized him. I had seen him that morning up in Villmark. Like Thorbjorn, he was wearing clothes to blend in with the Runde folk, but the knife that hung from his belt was pure Viking.

But the man who was following him to the patio was a Runde fisherman that had been at the Sorensen house that morning. He recognized me as well and gave me a little nod.

"What's going on here?" I whispered to Kara.

"What do you mean?" she asked.

"I'm seeing people from Villmark and people from Runde just mixing together," I said.

"Yes?"

"I thought that was against the rules?" I said. "Aren't you supposed to be a secret place? Hidden? And how come the Runde people don't seem to notice this isn't the building that exists during the day?"

Kara smiled at me then pointed across the room to where my grandmother was setting foaming mugs in front of two Runde women who were standing at her bar. "Your grandmother's magic. They don't notice the changes, and if you asked any of them tomorrow who they drank with tonight, they'll likely tell you it was a farmer from further up the gorge."

"There aren't that many farms, though," I said.

Kara shrugged. "Yeah, I think that's where the magic comes in. But don't worry about it. It's all perfectly safe. And fun!"

It made more sense now, my grandmother's urgency to get back down here. I wondered how hard the magic was that kept the Villmarkers at this party safely anonymous. Did she do this every night?

"Ingrid!" someone called. I looked around and noticed a waving motion from the far end of one of the tables. Loke was there with Andrew, and they were both waving for me to join them.

"I suppose I should go say hi," I said.

"We're here with a purpose," Thorbjorn said, scowling at Loke.

"Go say hi," Kara said, giving each of us a little push on the shoulder. She didn't move Thorbjorn an inch, but I nearly toppled over. She was stronger than she looked, and she looked plenty strong. "I don't see Roarr where I left him, but I'll ask around. I'll come get you when I find him."

"Thanks," I said, and waved back to Loke and Andrew. Thorbjorn was still scowling. "You can look for Roarr with Kara if you'd rather," I said.

"I'll stick with you," he said and followed me to the far end of the hall. Loke had cleared a spot for me on the bench between him and Andrew, and I just barely squeezed in.

"I was hoping you'd turn up," Andrew said, pulling an arm back so that his elbow wasn't in my way. "How are you liking Runde?"

I could scarcely admit that I'd barely been in Runde all day, and Loke was grinning at me like he knew that's what I was thinking.

"Very different from St. Paul, but I like it," I said.

"You never came back for the rest of your stuff," he said, a bit too loudly, but the room was loud. "I'd be happy to help you with it tomorrow if you'd like."

"That would be great!" I said.

Andrew smiled back at me then glanced up at Thorbjorn standing behind me. "Friend of yours?" he asked.

"We actually just met today," I said, leaning in close over the sticky table so that I wouldn't have to shout for Andrew to hear me. "Officially, that is. I saw him last night." It took a minute for my meaning to sink in, but I saw the confusion switch to comprehension.

"Your Viking!" he said, saluting Thorbjorn with his beer mug before taking a drink. Or, more accurately, another drink. I doubted it was his first beer.

"You can see my mistake," I said. Andrew tipped his head to one side as he considered Thorbjorn and then nodded.

"But why was he there?" he asked.

"Ingrid," Thorbjorn said, leaning over the table between Andrew and me to speak closer to my ear. It was loud in the hall, but I couldn't help feeling like putting his entire body between the two of us had been deliberate, and for an entirely different reason. "Kara is signaling us."

"I've got to go," I said to Andrew.

"Trouble?" Loke asked from my other side.

"Nothing we can't handle," Thorbjorn said.

"But we were going to buy you a drink," Andrew said. "Luke and I."

"Rain check?" I asked.

"Sure," he said.

I climbed back over the bench then followed Thorbjorn to where Kara was standing by the hall's open front doors. I could see more torches burning all around the parking lot, the light reflecting off the hoods of the pickups and cars that filled every available spot. I thought she was going to tell us what she had learned, but instead, she just turned and walked outside.

It was even colder than before, particularly with the wind blowing in from the lake.

"Where are we going?" I asked.

"Lisa's house," Kara said. "Your grandmother told me that Roarr just drank the one beer and then left through the front door."

"Did he say anything to her?" I asked.

"He didn't say anything to anyone," she said. "She's glad we're going to find him. She was considering doing it herself, and you know what that would do."

"No, actually," I said.

"None of us know that for sure," Thorbjorn said. "She never leaves the hall in the evenings. Never."

"Would the spells break if she did?" I asked.

Thorbjorn just shrugged, but Kara was more definite. "That must be what happens. Why else would she always be there?"

"Nora loves a party," Thorbjorn said. I couldn't tell if he was joking.

"If he didn't say anything, how do we know where he was going?" I asked.

"Where else would he go?" Kara asked.

"Either he's there, or he would've walked past it," Thorbjorn said before I could argue other theories. "And if he walked past it, Nilda would've seen him. I'm not absolutely sure where we're going. Ingrid, do you know the way?"

"It's just up there," I said, pointing past my grandmother's house to a few faintly winking lights barely visible through the trees.

I could've asked them to stop at my grandmother's house so I could grab a sweatshirt, but I didn't. There was a feeling of urgency growing in me, but it didn't feel like my own urgency. It was like the part of Lisa that I had touched out on the highway with Thorbjorn was still with me. Her worry for Roarr was strong, and whether I liked it or not, it was my worry too.

CHAPTER 17

We had just passed my grandmother's house when I heard the slap of feet running up the road behind us. I turned to see Andrew and Loke slow to a jog and then a walk as they reached us.

"We decided to tag along," Andrew said as he fell into step beside me.

"We?" Thorbjorn said, raising an eyebrow at Loke. Loke just shrugged, and Thorbjorn's scowl deepened. "We're not going to a party here. We're trying to find Roarr."

"Roarr was in the hall earlier," Loke said.

"Who's Roarr again?" Andrew asked, looking back towards the meeting hall as if that would give him a clue.

"Lisa's fiancé," I said. "We're going to the Sorensens. It's really not going to be a party."

"Lisa was engaged?" Andrew asked. "That's news to me."

"It was a secret love," Loke said with mock seriousness.

We reached the point where the Sorensens' front walk met the road. It was fully dark now, but I could see the shapes of two people coming down that walk towards the road. They stopped when they saw the group of us coming, and I could hear one of them sniffling softly.

"Hey," Andrew said in greeting. Then I realized it was Michelle and Jessica standing on the edge of the road. Jessica was dabbing at her eyes, and Michelle had an arm around her shoulders. His ebullient mood immediately down-shifted to concern. "Are you doing all right?" he asked.

"I've been better," Jessica said with a sigh. "We just stopped in to see if there was any news. This is so crazy. Did you hear they're investigating it as a murder now? Poison, they said. But who would poison Lisa? And why?"

Andrew was saying something to her in a comforting tone, but I stopped listening. I could see Nilda emerging from the trees just off the walk. She indicated with a little motion of her head that I should join her, and I edged closer to her.

"Anything?" I whispered to her.

"He was here," she whispered back, but she had inadvertently spoken during a lull in the other conversation, and now everyone was staring at us.

"Who was here?" Jessica asked.

"It's nothing," I said. "Nilda is just helping me with a... thing," I finished lamely.

Even in the dark, there was no mistaking the deep skepticism in Jessica's eyes. Michelle was looking at me with something like suspicion as well. Andrew just looked confused.

"Say, guys," Loke said. "Andrew and I were just heading up to the meeting hall to have a drink in Lisa's memory. But we didn't know her as well as you did. Won't you join us? Without you, we're going to run out of Lisa stories way too fast."

"We're going back to the hall?" Andrew asked in a too-loud whisper, and Loke poked him hard with his elbow. "Yeah. We were."

"I don't know," Jessica said, shaking her head.

"Come on," Michelle said. "Just one drink? Otherwise, you're just going to sit alone in that café and stare at the walls."

"We'll get you home safely after," Andrew said. "Promise."

"All right," Jessica said, then mustered a weak smile. "Actually, that sounds really good. It was so sad in there with her parents. I'd really like to remember the fun side of Lisa."

They headed up the road back the way we'd come, Michelle still with an arm around Jessica, Andrew already in the middle of some story beside her. Loke trailed a half a step behind them, hands in his pockets and the cold lake wind in his hair. He turned to look back at us and very clearly mouthed the words, "you owe me."

"Was he talking to you or me?" I asked Thorbjorn.

"Knowing Loke? Both," he said. Then he asked, "so who's this Andrew?"

"I don't really know," I said. "He was there last night after I crashed the car. I guess his dad runs the service station, but I don't know what he does. Something with wood, maybe."

"With wood?"

"Well, he always smells like wood, and last night I saw these little shavings caught in his sweater and also sawdust, so I just thought..." I trailed off, realizing I was going on about the way one man smelled to another, and he really didn't seem to like it.

"Guys," Kara said to get our attention. We clustered closer to Nilda and Kara. I didn't know if we still needed to whisper now that we seemed alone, but I appreciated being able to use Thorbjorn's bulk as a wind barrier.

"He was here," Nilda said again. "Roarr."

"Did he make a scene?" I asked.

"No, he never actually went in," she said. "He came to here, just about where we're standing, but then he stopped. I think he was of two minds. Half of him wanted to go in and do what, I have no idea. But the other half wasn't so sure. So he just paced here and mumbled to himself."

"Mumbled, like talking? He came out of the catatonia?" I asked.

"Well, I couldn't hear him. It could've been nonsense noises," Nilda said. "He didn't seem well. But he was moving around on his own, so I guess that's an improvement."

"But where did he go?" Thorbjorn asked.

"I'm not done telling you," Nilda said. "So he was pacing here and mumbling to himself, and it looked like he'd finally decided to come in. He even started up the walk with a determined look on his face. But then all of a sudden, he just stopped. Like, in mid-step. His foot was just hovering off the paving stone like this." Nilda mimed a freeze-frame of a person walking.

"Like a spell?" I asked.

"You know spells are pretty much just something your grandmother can do," Thorbjorn said. "It's a rare skill."

"No, I don't know," I sighed. "Really, no one else?"

"Halldis dabbles," Kara said. "But your grandmother would never take her on as an apprentice."

"Because she's evil?" I asked.

"I told you-" Thorbjorn started to say.

"I know, I know," I interrupted. "She's off, is all I'm saying."

"I don't think she has this sort of power anyway," Kara said. "She makes herself look younger all the time. That's draining. She also puts a whammy on top of that, to be absolutely sure that she's the most attractive woman around."

"Yeah, I got hit with that," I said.

"But freezing someone?" Kara shook her head. Then she looked at her sister. "But what happened?"

"He just stood there, and I debated coming out of hiding to see what was wrong with him," Nilda said. "But then the wind died down, and I could smell this odor. I don't know what it was. It seemed like something I had smelled before, lots of times, but when I tried to put a name to it, I couldn't."

"Where was it coming from?" Thorbjorn asked.

"I don't know," Nilda said, and she was hugging herself now. "I'm sorry. I know I should've gone out and figured out what was happening. But something about it was... scaring me. I was scared." She bit down on her lip, and although I'd only known her for a few hours, I could sense that it cost her something to admit that.

I wondered what she had smelled that had been familiar, frightening, and unnameable all at once?

"It's all right," Thorbjorn said. "It's a clue all the same; it might help later. Where's Roarr now?"

"I don't know exactly," Nilda said. "But after a minute or two standing like a statue, he turned and started walking back up towards the meeting hall. But it was like he was fighting the urge every step of the way. He wasn't going very fast, and it was just before those two women came out of the Sorensen house. I'm actually surprised you didn't pass him on the road on your way here."

"We didn't see him," I said.

"It sounded like he was possessed or ensorcelled or something when he left here," Kara said. "Would someone in that sort of state even be able to hide from us?"

"We need to talk to Nora," Thorbjorn said.

We walked back to the meeting hall. I wasn't sure how we were going to get my grandmother's attention without Jessica, Andrew, and the others noticing us, but as we crossed the parking lot, I saw her standing just outside the doors, waiting for us.

"Did you see him? Roarr?" I asked her.

"No, but something is definitely going on," she said. She had her arms crossed tightly and a deep glower on her face.

"Is it Halldis? Is she doing some sort of magic?" I asked.

"No, this is far outside her power," she said. "And it doesn't have the feel of her magic. I'm very familiar with her patterns, and this isn't hers."

"Is there anyone else in the village who could do this?" Kara asked, but Thorbjorn was already shaking his head.

"No. It must come from beyond," he said.

"Are you talking about from those mountains that are in old Norway?" I asked.

"I don't like to entertain the thought either, but I don't see another solution," my grandmother said to Thorbjorn.

"I've failed," he said. "I let something slip through."

"Let's not jump to any conclusions just yet," my grandmother said. "I can't leave here until midnight. I'm afraid you are on your own until then. What's your plan?"

"We've been trying to find Roarr all night," I said.

"He wasn't at the Sorensens house? I thought for sure that was where he was heading," she said.

"He was, but he never went in. He was pulled away by some sort of spell," Nilda said.

"Maybe that's what you felt happening," I said. "But we didn't see him, and he should've walked right by us."

"He didn't come back here," my grandmother said, shaking her head.

"We're assuming he was going home," Thorbjorn said. "What if he wasn't?"

My grandmother's chin dropped to her chest as she mulled over her own thoughts. Then she looked up at me as if assessing me.

"Ingrid, stay with Nilda and Kara in Villmark," she said at last. "They'll keep you safe."

"Wouldn't I be safer with you?" I asked.

"Not here. This is an in-between place. I know you don't understand, and now isn't the time to explain. You just have to trust me," she said.

"Of course I trust you, mormor," I said. "But what about Thorbjorn?"

"I have something else I have to tend to," he said. "Nilda and Kara can protect you as well as I can."

"I'm not worried about *me*," I said. "But all this talk of protection is starting to freak me out a little. What's going on that you're not telling me?"

"We'll explain what we can," Nilda said, looping her arm through mine. "Once we're safe. Within the spells that protect Villmark, and within the spells that protect our own house. Kara and I will tell you everything we can."

"Slumber party," Kara said, pumping her hands in the air, but her attempt at levity was met with stony silence, and she dropped her hands again.

"I'll be there shortly after midnight," my grandmother said, catching my hand and squeezing it. "Now, hurry."

Then she turned and went back inside the meeting hall, and we took the path that circled around it. Back up that treacherous waterfall path, and this time by moonlight.

CHAPTER 18

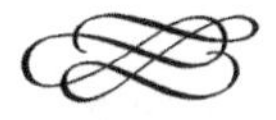

The village by night was really charming, the moon reflecting off the cobblestones. Every garden gate was flanked by a pair of electric lights, bright enough to show the way in but not so bright that they interfered with the night sky. I supposed muggings weren't a worry here.

And yet the warmth and cheeriness that radiated from the windows of the homes around me didn't reach my heart. I felt oddly detached from it, like it was a refreshing summer rain, and I was wearing full-body rain gear.

"Ingrid? Are you doing all right?" Kara asked. I looked up to see the three of them had already reached the village square, but I was lagging behind.

"I thought we'd find Roarr by now," I said. "It feels like we should have."

"He was moving slowly when I saw him, but that doesn't mean he didn't pick up the pace later," Nilda said. "We'll find him."

"What do you mean by 'feels?'" Thorbjorn asked me with a serious look in his eyes.

I shook my head. "I don't know. Something has been lingering in my mind since we were on the crossroads where Lisa passed," I said. "Maybe I'm just tired, though. It's been a long day."

"Do you feel anything more specific?" he asked. "See if you can."

I closed my eyes and quieted my mind. It reached a tranquil state far faster than I was used to, but even so, nothing rose to the surface. I opened my eyes and shook my head. "Sorry. Nothing."

"Watch her closely," he said to Nilda and Kara. "I have to go," he said to me.

"I know you do," I said. "I'll be fine."

"Keep her safe," he said, making eye contact with first Nilda and then Kara. They both nodded gravely, but the moment he was out of earshot, they exchanged a glance with each other, and while they didn't exactly break out in smiles, the grimness that had settled over everything lightened up just a touch.

"We should get indoors," Nilda said, sliding an arm through mine. Kara did the same on my other side, and we three walked down the road that led to the south, to the public garden.

"I still feel strange," I confessed.

Kara gave my arm a squeeze. "Maybe that's just part of being home again. Like it's starting to sink in for you."

"Did I know either of you when I was eight?" I asked.

"We saw you around," Kara said, looking across me at Nilda, who nodded her agreement.

"You stayed close to your grandmother most of the time," Nilda said.

"Unless she was busy, in which case she left you with Gunna," Kara said. "She's the mother of the Thors. And then you and Thorbjorn would sneak away, and there'd be a ruckus until you were found."

"I really wished I remembered that," I said.

"It'll come back to you," Kara said. She sounded more confident than I felt. After the constant rush of memories that had plagued me all morning, I hadn't felt a single twinge of memory since.

Suddenly we stopped walking, all of us at once.

"What's that smell?" Kara asked. "I can just barely catch it, but it's driving me crazy. What is it?"

"I know what this is," Nilda said. She was also sniffing the air and released my arm as she took a few steps away from me, like she was following a scent. "This is what I smelled before when I was watching Roarr. You see what I mean? I know what this is, but I can't name it."

Then I smelled it too. I felt like the smell wanted to bring memories back. I could see myself as a child, but the memory never extended to anything with context. I didn't even know how old of a child I was in that half-formed memory. Where had I smelled this smell before? What had I been doing?

It was just on the tip of my tongue, so maddening. Nilda was still walking a step or two at a time, smelling the air as if hunting down the source. Kara was doing the same but in the opposite direction. I remained in the middle of the road, closing my eyes to try to quiet my mind. But my mind was already quiet. I had no fear, no sense of alarm. This was strange - the people meant to be protecting me wandering away should be alarming - but that sense of familiarity was so strong. Nothing that familiar to me could be a bad thing, could it?

I opened my eyes and found that Nilda and Kara were both gone. I was alone. I opened my mouth to call out to them, but nothing came out.

Well, that was okay. I was perfectly safe.

I started walking down the middle of the road, following the line of reflected moonlight ahead of me. At first, I thought I was going back to the gardens. Maybe I'd go inside the greenhouse this time, see what was in there for myself. Was that what I was smelling? A growing things smell?

That feeling like I was about to remember something strobed bright - I had it! - but then dimmed again. No, I didn't have it. But it was so close.

Then I found myself standing still. I had turned away from the gardens and was facing a break in the fences between two houses.

And between the two, I could see warm firelight glowing from out of the doorway of Halldis' house. The round red door stood wide open, the glow from that fire lighting the front step more inviting than any doormat.

Then the comforting smell drifted away, just for a moment, and that smothering blanket of safe feeling fell away. Panic shrieked in my mind, but I still couldn't make it come out of my mouth, not even as an inarticulate scream. And then the smell was back and my feet were moving again, walking me up that path between the fences towards that house.

I was right. Halldis was behind everything. I knew it!

But being right wasn't going to save me in that moment. I tried again to call out, but I couldn't even open my mouth, let alone make a sound. I tried to stop my feet, then to reach out and catch hold of the slats of the fences on either side of me, but I was powerless.

I could close my eyes. That was it.

I tried to quiet my mind, but my growing panic wasn't going to let that happen. For some reason, the only thought I could focus on was Mjolner. Where had that cat gotten to? If he was somewhere I had just zombie-walked past, had he seen me? Would he be able to get help?

I focused everything on that thought, trying to telepathically summon my cat and send him for help. But while I knew he could walk through walls and was half-convinced he could speak if he chose to, I had never seen any signs that he was telepathic.

I felt a blast of warm air on my face and opened my eyes. I was in Halldis' hut now, walking towards the firepit at its center. The cooking pots were gone now, and the fire blazed almost dangerously high. The herbs drying from the rafters were smoking as they spun in the hot air. Was that the source of the smell?

No, I didn't think it was. That would smeller cleaner then what lingered in my nose. But what was it?

Then I heard the door slam shut behind me. I had stopped walking, but I still wasn't free. I couldn't turn to see, but I was certain there was someone standing behind me.

"Have a seat, Ingrid Torfudottir," Halldis said, and stepped into view. She was showing me to a chair with a polite smile, as if I had called for tea. As if we were friends. "And I shall continue to speak English with you, as it's all you know. So many of our young people speak it half the time now. I don't approve. But for you I must make an exception."

I sat down on the chair. It was far too close to the fire, uncomfortably hot, and the thick smoke was making my head swim.

"Now, I suppose you're wondering why I invited you here this evening?" Halldis asked as she smoothed the back of her skirt before sitting on a chair across from mine, a more comfortable distance from the fire. The smoke-filled the entire hut, but it didn't seem to bother her at all. "In truth, you're not my only guest. I'm just waiting for the other to come. She'll be along as quickly as she can. As quickly as she can after midnight, of course. You do know about midnight, don't you?"

I couldn't answer. She knew I couldn't answer. And yet she looked at me with her eyebrows raised in expectation of my response.

"You know, I don't think you do," she decided, leaning back in her chair and crossing her legs then smoothing out her snowy white skirt again. "I'm sure Nora intended to explain it all to you at some point. I'm so glad she left you to run loose in the meantime. I mean, how lovely of her! You, out in the open. Unprotected. What did she think would happen?"

I narrowed my eyes. It was all I could do. I hoped I was shooting daggers at her, but for all I knew, I was drooling, which would really undercut the message.

My whole body had gone tingly and numb.

"Ooh, such anger!" she said, slapping her hands together as if amused. "I suppose you thought Thorbjorn was some sort of protection? Well, maybe he is, against bears and wolves or even trolls. But those are not the dangers that will gather around the likes of you, and she knew that. She knew it!"

She sat back and grew quiet for a moment, staring into the flames as if lost in thought. "She's made many bad decisions, your grandmother," she went on, more calmly now. "And I don't mean just never taking me seriously. She may have inherited the gift of Torfa's line, but she misuses it. Gathering together and drinking with the fishermen? That's not what magic is for. No, when I take my place on that dais, things will be different. You'll see."

I, of course, said nothing. But I was annoyed, deeply annoyed. All of this, whatever spell she put on Nilda and Kara to lead them astray and on me to bring me here, it was all about some apprenticeship she resented my grandmother not giving her?

So Thorbjorn had been right about Halldis all along.

And now I was trapped here until she let me go or my grandmother came to get me. Trapped, not able to help find Lisa's murderer. Not that I was much help with that, but still. This was a distraction I didn't need.

And frankly, I still didn't entirely understand. Halldis seemed like she'd taught herself magic quite proficiently. What was the point in apprenticing under anyone's tutelage for her now?

Then from behind me, I heard a knock on the door. Just a single knock, and then the sound of the door opening. Just like my grandmother always did it. Halldis glanced past me and saw whoever had just joined us. Then she looked back at me and must've seen what I was thinking in my eyes, because she laughed.

"Oh, you thought it was your grandmother here to rescue you?" she asked. "No, dear. It's not quite time for that. Even for you, Nora Torfudottir won't risk letting the spells fall apart. You'll just have to wait. But now we won't have to wait alone."

Then she was looking past me again, gesturing to whoever was standing behind me. "Come in, Roarr, and shut that door. We're trying to keep the smoke in, remember?" She was still speaking English, I supposed for my benefit.

Then I heard the door behind me shut. The stone sliding over the cave entrance behind the waterfall hadn't sounded so final.

CHAPTER 19

Now I was really confused. Why was Roarr of all people coming in the door?

But of course, Nilda had smelled the same thing in the air when he had walked away from Lisa Sorensen's house as we'd all smelled when I was lured away. Two people could be using the same spell on the same evening but targeting different people, but it didn't seem likely.

Still, what did Halldis want with Roarr?

Then he walked past me, and I flinched on the inside. Did I look like that? All blank and zombie-like?

"Have a seat, Roarr," Halldis said, getting up so he could take her chair. He did as he was told, but his eyes never left Halldis'. They were full of raw emotion, pleading at her to do something.

"You have something to say?" Halldis asked him, then turned away from him, her arms crossed as she scowled. She was still speaking English, and I felt like I was watching some kind of play she was performing just for me. "I don't know why I should hear you out. I really don't. But all right."

She made no move, not so much as a gesture, and she spoke no magic words, but suddenly Roarr could speak. He heaved in breath after breath, bending forward as he did so. It was like he was tied to the chair, unable to move anything below his neck, and I knew whatever Halldis had done had freed him to speak but only to speak.

"I've done everything you asked," he said when he had his breath back. "Everything. And still, you don't trust me?"

"Of course I don't trust you," Halldis said, spinning around to face him. "I've had to push you every step of the way. If I stop pushing for a minute, you break down completely. What is there for me to trust in that? You came so close to letting me down. So close."

"I've done everything for you," he said. "But it's never enough."

"You've done everything for *us*," she snapped.

"No, for you," he said. Then he swallowed hard before saying, "I don't matter. You know I don't."

"Obviously, you matter. Don't be silly," she said, but her harsh tone had softened, and her posture was loosening up as well. She uncrossed her arms and waved a gesture in his direction. Roarr fell forward, hands on his knees, and panted for breath again.

It did feel confining, this spell of hers. It was like my whole body had gone to sleep. The pins and needles were going to be killer.

"Well?" Halldis asked leadingly. "Nothing to report? Still, it's like pulling teeth with you. Always so much work. Were you on the edge of the village just now or not?"

"You know I was," Roarr said sullenly. Now that he could move, he was twisting his body on the chair so that he wasn't facing Halldis, who was pacing up and down by the foot of her bed.

"Well?" she prompted again.

"I saw. They all went out there," Roarr said. "All five of them."

"Just like I said they would," Halldis said triumphantly. "And their father?"

"I didn't see him," Roarr said.

Halldis waved a hand dismissively. "Well, he doesn't matter. He's not strong enough to stop us once his sons are gone. And you'll soon replace him on the council."

"I don't even know if I want that anymore," Roarr said. "None of this is like how you said it would be."

"I know you're upset," she said, but the heavy sigh that accompanied that spoke more of growing impatience than of empathy.

"I'm not upset," he said. "I'm... nothing. Empty, maybe? I should be feeling something, shouldn't I?"

"Do you really want to?" Halldis asked. "Do you want to feel it? All the grief? Do you want me to give it back to you?" She was holding out a cupped hand, like she kept all of his grief there resting on the palm of her hand.

"Why did she have to die? You said we could be together if she promised to stay here. She was going to promise. Just like I told you. Why did she have to die like that?" he asked. And it really was like Halldis held all of his grief and sadness in her hand. He just sounded confused, not sad. And yet he could only be talking about Lisa.

"She didn't have to die," Halldis said. She stopped pacing to come around the fire and slip her arms around him from behind, pressing her cheek against his shoulder. "She wasn't supposed to die. It just happened. And we did the best we could with what was left behind."

“Please don’t touch me again. Not now,” he said, but she didn’t move away and in the end neither did he. “But why was she even here?" he went on. "Why did she come here at all?"

"I don't know, dear," Halldis said. "It was an accident. Put it out of your mind."

Then she looked at me, holding my gaze as she hugged him tightly. But something was going on with the hands she held clasped over his stomach. Something was glowing there. Then her entire body was glowing. It wasn't bright. In fact, it was so dim I almost thought I imagined it.

Almost. But I felt something happening. I felt it in my bones. She was doing something to Roarr. And she was looking at me the entire time, making sure I saw it.

"I just can't do that again," Roarr said, putting his hands over hers on his stomach. "It was too much."

"I know, I know," she murmured. "You'll never have to. I swear it. We're nearly there, aren't we?"

"I guess so," he said.

“Come here,” she said. I wanted to scream at Roarr, to tell him to run. Didn’t he feel what she was doing to him? Didn’t he know it was just another spell?

But I couldn’t scream. He did hesitate, for a moment. But then he turned around in her arms and kissed her.

I did the only thing I could do. I closed my eyes. I couldn't shut out the sounds, though. And they went on for far too long.

"Roarr," Halldis said. "Stop. It's nearly midnight."

"What's midnight?" he asked, still kissing her between words.

"My appointment with Nora," Halldis said. "We have to be ready."

"Nora?" Roarr said. I opened my eyes to see him looking right at me. The color drained from his face, and he was gaping at me like he hadn't even realized I was there. "Why is *she* here?"

"You know why," Halldis said.

"To lure Nora here? Then what happens to her?" he asked.

Halldis shrugged. "Does it really matter?"

"Yes, it matters," Roarr said. The blood was coming back to his face in a dark rush. "I'm not moving any more bodies, Halldis. You promised no more bodies!"

"I'm not planning to kill her," Halldis said with a laugh. "I don't even need to kill Nora. I just need to break her a little."

"I don't want her involved," Roarr said, pointing a jabbing finger at me. "Let her go."

"I'm sorry?" Halldis said in a dangerous voice. "Are you giving me orders now?"

"No, I..." he broke off, flustered, and she stepped back up to him to rest a hand on his cheek.

"This will all be over soon," she said. "The pain will end. Your grief will end."

He had been calming under her touch, but his anger returned when she said the word "grief." He pushed her away, and she stumbled over the hem of her skirt, nearly falling into the fire.

"You made me put the woman I love in the crossroads!" he yelled at her. "And you lied to me! She wasn't dead. She was still alive when I left her there. You knew she was alive when you told me to carry her away. And *you* could've saved her."

"Be careful what you say, especially in English," Halldis said, then pointed a finger at me. "You're condemning her to death with your words."

Roarr looked at me, and again it was like he hadn't known I was there. But this time, the shocked look he gave me melted to confusion and then grief. He pressed his hands over his face. "I've got to get out of here. This damned smoke. I can't think."

"Don't open that door," Halldis hissed. But he was already halfway there. She lunged after him, both of them passing out of my view. I heard the door open, but only for an instant. Then it was slammed shut again.

"Let me pass," Roarr growled.

"Don't leave me," she pleaded. Was she going to try to put her whammy on him again? She seemed to be getting diminishing returns on that. "Come back to the fire, and let's talk. Let's decide what we're going to do next together."

Their voices dropped lower then. I couldn't make out the words, but her tone was still pleading and pouting by turns. And his sharp, short answers were softening.

Then I felt several sharp points stabbing into my thighs. At first, I thought the spell was breaking, that the numbness was becoming pins and needles. But the yelp of pain that tried to escape me remained trapped at the back of my throat. I was still paralyzed.

But then I looked down to see Mjolner on my lap, his claws buried deep into my legs. He was looking up at my face like all of this was just a ploy to get my attention. How I wished I could tell him what I thought of his methods.

I put it all into my eyes and hoped he got the message.

But the moment my eyes met his, I felt something change. The magic binding me fell away.

I was free.

CHAPTER 20

The spell was gone, but I still couldn't move. If Halldis saw me moving, she would just find another way to bind me. I'm sure she knew worse ways.

So I had to keep sitting as still as possible. Which was really hard because those pins and needles were all over my body now, and my lungs longed for me to suck in air the way Roarr had.

Roarr and Halldis were still behind me. Between me and the only way out. They were still murmuring at each other as before. Nothing I had done so far had tipped them off. Then finally they started to move. I heard the rustle of Halldis' skirt and the clunk of Roarr's boots. Then Halldis came into view, walking backward as she towed Roarr after her, his hand in both of hers. She was smiling at him, and her skin had that glow of dewy youth to it again.

I thought I was doing a good job, not moving, not even my eyes. But suddenly, Halldis lunged at me, putting a hand on the back of the chair over my shoulder as she leaned right into my face.

"Did you think I didn't notice?" she asked me. She was grinning at me, but in a flash that transformed into a look of pure rage. She snatched Mjolner up off my lap, holding him by the scruff of his neck to dangle him before my eyes. "Did you think I didn't see?!?"

"Halldis?" Roarr asked.

"Put him down," I said. Now I couldn't move because I was too terrified. She had murder in her eyes and my cat in her hands. I would never be able to move fast enough to save him.

"Halldis, it's not midnight yet," Roarr said in a deliberately reasonable voice. "It's not time yet. Just leave her."

"How did I lose control?" Halldis asked, although I couldn't tell who she was talking to. Maybe herself. She straightened up and clutched Mjolner tight in her arms. "I'm losing control of Roarr, losing control of the wards that protect this place. How did you get in here?" She turned Mjolner around in her hands to look him in the eye, as if she too thought he could speak but chose not to.

He still chose not to, but he had other ways of getting his point across. He spread the six toes of his right front paw wide and then slashed them across Halldis' face. She shrieked as she threw him to the ground and bent double, her hands pressed to her face. I sprung up from the chair with a cry, but there was no sign of Mjolner. I dropped to my hands and knees to look under the bed, but he wasn't there either. Where had he gone?

I felt fingers winding into my hair, but before I could move away, they tightened into a fist. I was dragged back to my feet by my hair and looked up into the bleeding face of Halldis.

"The thing is, I can always get things back under my control," she hissed at me. "That's what I *do*."

"I have no trouble believing you're a control freak," I said, "but you're definitely losing it."

"Am I?" she said. She still had one hand tangled in my hair, but with the other, she pointed back to where Roarr was creeping up behind her. "Sit down!" she demanded.

That zombie look came over his face again, and he collapsed into the chair. He sat so rigidly I knew he was bound just as I had been.

As much as she had never looked back at him, she had still been distracted by using magic to bind him even if just for half a second. But half a second was all I needed. I punched her in the nose. Hard.

I'd never punched anyone before. I could only assume I had

somehow done it incorrectly as my hand suddenly exploded in pain. But she had released my hair before she fell back, and I was once again free.

But still trapped in the house. That hadn't changed.

I ran for the door, but she was faster. Way faster; she must've used magic. One moment she was behind me clutching her bleeding nose, and the next, she was just a blur of white shooting past me to end up with her back to the door and her arms thrown wide, blocking my way.

"Get out of my way," I said.

"Or what?" Halldis asked.

Good question. My throbbing hand was saying pretty strongly that throwing more fists was out of the question. But what else did I have?

I picked up the chair.

"Really?" Halldis said with a laugh. "You're just proving my point. How can Nora take you on as an apprentice? You have all the subtlety of one of the Thors." Then her voice dropped low to growl, "you have no magic at all."

"Probably not," I agreed.

"Whereas I have more magic than your grandmother ever knew," Halldis said. She pointed at the chair in my hands, and I yelped as it exploded into shards of wood. I was sprayed with the shrapnel, slivers driving into me everywhere.

"You can't stop me," she said as she pointed another finger at the fire, and it roared to double its size. I danced away before the flames could reach me, but barely. I could smell singed hair and was pretty sure it was mine.

"What are you going to do?" she asked. She was raising both arms now, and I didn't know what she planned to do next, but I really didn't want to find out.

Then I saw a flash of movement. Mjolner was darting out from under the worktable where he had been hiding, running straight towards me. I bent to scoop him up. I was just straightening with him in my arms when Halldis hurled her spell at me. I flinched, shutting my eyes, but had no time to dodge out of the way.

Then I opened my eyes. Nothing had happened.

Except Mjolner in my arms was making crackling noises. I looked down to see little electric shocks shooting through his fur but quickly dissipating. He didn't seem hurt, just… staticky.

"What do you have that I don't?" Halldis raged on, apparently unaware of what had just happened. "What do you have? Nothing!"

"I have a cat," I said, still looking deep into Mjolnir's greenish-yellow eyes.

"A cat?" she repeated incredulously. "I draw power from the deepest well. I wield magics that were old when this world began. But you have a cat?"

I didn't say anything, which only seemed to enrage her more. She lifted her hands high, and I could see the power coalescing there in shimmering spheres that kept growing in size and intensity.

"Mjolner?" I said to my cat. He blinked at me.

Then I had a sudden image in my head. But I didn't like it at all.

"No," I said to him.

"Meow," he said. And really, there was no arguing with him.

Even if I wanted to, there was no time. Halldis had drawn in all the power she could, and her hands were moving now, moving to aim her spell at me.

"Please be safe," I said.

Then I thrust Mjolner out, holding him at arm's length. As if his tiny body could possibly be a shield.

And yet it was. Her spell hit him dead on. I saw those little bolts of lightning dancing through his fur again, but the larger part of her power was deflected straight up into the air. It hit the peaked ceiling where the chimney was and blew off half the roof. I looked up and saw stars twinkling back down at me through the fire smoke.

Then I pulled Mjolner close again. Not only did he seem unharmed, he was actually purring.

"That was interesting," Halldis said, looking up at the stars. Her magic still lingered like a pillar of purplish-white light that stabbed straight up into the sky, into infinity.

"Mjolner protects me from your magic," I said as I stroked the cat in my arms. "You can destroy the rest of your place testing that, or you can just take my word for it."

"Where did you find such a beast?" she asked.

"He found me," I said.

That stumped her for a moment, but then she let the confusion go with a shrug. I could see her drawing power again, although more slowly than last time.

"We're going to do this all night?" I asked.

"However long it takes," she said.

"All right. I'm ready," I said. But this time, when I held Mjolner aloft, he squirmed out of my grasp. He hit the ground running, back under the worktable.

"You were saying?" Halldis asked, still building her power.

Someone started pounding on the door behind her, or maybe two someones, but it sounded like something happening very far away.

"I was saying we don't have to do this," I said, holding up my hands as if they could somehow ward her magic away.

"Years of planning just went up in smoke. Decades! If there's no way out of this for me, there's no way out of this for you," she said. Then her hands started to move, to aim her spell at me.

I looked around for something to use for cover, but there was nothing. Then I saw a blur of motion. Mjolner, on the run again. I dropped to one knee and held out my hands to catch him.

But he wasn't heading to me. He zipped right past me, launching himself into the air to land on Roarr's lap.

Then the spell hit me, knocking me to the ground.

It was like fire all over my body. I lost all awareness of the rest of the world around me. There was nothing but that fire.

CHAPTER 21

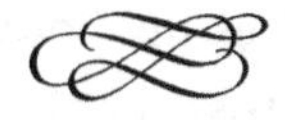

I curled up on my side and pulled my knees close to my chest. I wanted to put my arms over my head, to tuck myself into a tighter ball, but everywhere any part of my body touched anything at all was agony. I felt those electric jolts dancing all over me.

Then those jolts slowed their velocity and intensity. I still couldn't get up, and I didn't even want to open my eyes.

But I could hear someone still pounding on that red door. Help was so close, but it couldn't get to me. So I would just have to find a way to get to it.

I peered out through the bare slits my eyes would open to. Halldis still stood in my way. She was summoning more power, but it was building even more slowly than last time. She was looking older, too, her hair hanging limply around her face, and her snowy white gown now more of a gray. Was she losing her magic or just concentrating it all on me? I thought maybe it was both. She was so vain, it had to be both.

Still, given that I had yet to move from where she had left me pounded to the floor, the mad grin of confidence in her own inevitable victory didn't exactly feel misplaced.

Then I felt something raspy on my hand. Mjolner. He was back, licking me with his cat tongue. But where was Roarr?

I heard Halldis yelp. I looked back to the door just in time to see Halldis get tackled to the ground by Roarr. The power she had been gathering discharged into the air as she fell. It made a loud crack like a cannon firing. It felt like it popped my eardrums, but that was nothing compared to the burning feeling from before.

I tried to get to my feet, but my body was shaking too much, so I just started pulling myself across the floor towards the door. Mjolner saw what I was doing and sauntered past me to sit down to the side of the doormat, out of the way of the door should it suddenly burst open. Halldis and Roarr were still wrestling with each other on the other side of the doormat, but Mjolner ignored them. He merely raised one over-sized paw and smacked it against the red door.

Which promptly sprung open, spilling Thorbjorn and Loke into the room. They blinked dazedly for a moment. Then Loke's eyes met mine down on the floor at the same moment that Thorbjorn saw Halldis and Roarr.

Loke came to my side to help me sit up while Thorbjorn reached into the tumble of bodies near him. I imagined he was trying to do what he had done at the meeting hall, grabbing each of them by the collar and pulling them apart. He got Roarr, but Halldis in her wispy gown eluded his grasp. She did that fast-moving thing like a blur of grayish-white and then came to a halt at the far end of the cabin, the fire between her and the rest of us.

"Ingrid?" Loke said.

"I'm okay," I said. "Where's my grandmother?"

"Still down below," he said. "It's not midnight yet."

"We can't take Halldis without her," I said.

"Please. *I* can take Halldis," he said with that insane smile of his.

"Then come and get me," Halldis said. She was standing over one of her wooden chests. The lid was thrown back, and she was sliding bronze gauntlets over her forearms. She grinned at Loke then clapped them together. Suddenly she had a sword in one hand and a hammer in the other. Both looked like they were made of golden light, but I could tell by the grin on her face that they would feel all too real if she struck any of us with them.

"Get behind me," Thorbjorn said. Loke pulled me to my feet and moved me towards the door then took the spear Thorbjorn was holding out for him. Then Thorbjorn took the sword and ax from his belt. With a nod, they split up, one moving around each side of the fire.

I didn't like the way Halldis was still grinning as she waited for them to reach her. Like she knew something none of the rest of us did.

"Wait!" Roarr cried, pushing Loke out of the way as he ran to Halldis' side. Halldis held out the sword as if to ward him off.

"Get back," she told him.

"But my place is between you and danger," he said. "Always. I swore to that."

"You swore to lots of things," she said dismissively.

"And I'll keep every promise, if you'll let me," he said. "I know I've lost my way. It's been a hard couple of days. But the future is still us together, right? You and me?"

She looked at him skeptically, not lowering her weapons. But not attacking either.

"What is going on?" Thorbjorn whispered over his shoulder to me. Like I could sum that up in a hurry.

"The fire," Loke said, which made no sense to me.

But before I could ask, our attention was back on Halldis and Roarr, because she had lowered her sword arm, and he was kissing her again. Thorbjorn darted forward, hoping to take advantage of her guard being down, but even in the clinch, she was aware of his approach. She extended the hammer and tapped him gently in the center of his chest. He staggered back like he'd been hit with a swinging wrecking ball.

He recovered quickly, but Halldis was ready for him with sword and hammer both. Thorbjorn looked down at the weapons in his own hands, and I could see him working out what would be the best strategy.

"Roarr, get that spear from the weak one," Halldis said.

"Hey," Loke protested.

Roarr turned to look at Halldis. "As you wish," he said.

She spared him a brief smile then turned her attention back to Thorbjorn.

But Roarr didn't move towards Loke. Instead, he reached up and pulled something off of Halldis' neck. He stepped back with it clenched tightly in his hand.

She gasped, and the golden hammer disappeared as she pressed that hand to her throat. Then she made a choking sound and fell to her knees, the sword disappearing.

"What did you do?" she said. She was on her hands and knees now, her hair hiding her face from view. It was looking stringier than ever, and there was something wrong with her voice. It sounded broken, all of its melody gone.

"Thorbjorn," Loke said, "get that rain barrel from the garden. We have to put this fire out. I've got her."

"Yeah," Thorbjorn agreed, putting his weapons back on his belt. He looked down at Halldis still gasping on the floor then ran to get the barrel.

"So what *did* you do?" Loke asked Roarr. Roarr opened his hand and then tipped it. There was a leather cord twisted in his fingers, and dangling from that cord was a bronze amulet. I couldn't quite tell what it was meant to represent, but it looked very old.

"I took her power," Roarr said. "She always wears this. She does rituals with it deep in the mountains at some place she's never let me see. Every time she comes back from a ritual she has more power than before."

"I've never seen that before," Thorbjorn said as he came back in the door.

"She wears it under her clothes," Roarr said.

"But how did you-" Thorbjorn started to ask, but then just shook his head. "Never mind. We'll know everything soon enough." Then he upended the barrel over the bonfire.

I hadn't realized until that moment that I had been smelling that familiar yet strange smell the entire time. I had stopped noticing it shortly after coming inside the cabin. But as the fire died, the concentration of that odor increased tenfold, and we were all choking.

"Outside, outside," Loke said. He pushed me out ahead of him and didn't stop pushing me until we were across the entire length of the garden. Roarr was there with us, as was Mjolner. It took another minute for Thorbjorn to join us, dragging Halldis with him. She wasn't resisting exactly. It was more like she'd suddenly grown too weak to walk without assistance.

"What was that?" I asked.

"Henbane, among other things," Loke said. "Of course its use is strictly forbidden," he added, bending down to try to look Halldis in her face. But she was still hiding behind the curtain of her white hair.

Wait, white hair?

"What does henbane do?" I asked.

"It concentrates magic," my grandmother said as she emerged from between the two fences. Thorbjorn tightened his grip on Halldis as she tried to pull away from him. "Especially magic that influences minds."

Halldis tossed her hair back out of her face, and I gasped out loud. She looked decades older, maybe even centuries. Her face was as lined as a dried crabapple, and not just around the eyes. And she hadn't been faking her sudden frailty; her body looked thin and brittle, and her spine had a curve to it that wouldn't straighten out even as she tried to draw herself up to nose to nose with my grandmother.

"What do you know of it?" she croaked at my grandmother. "You who would never deign to touch such things."

"Every magic has a use," my grandmother said. "And every magic has a price."

"That's why she looks so old? Because of the magic?" I asked.

"She looks old because she is old," my grandmother said. "I could always see it. No, she paid the price in other ways."

"She had this," Roarr said, stepping forward to put the amulet into my grandmother's hand. She looked genuinely shocked to see it. But when she looked up at Roarr again, he started to weep. "I'm so sorry. So sorry."

"Not here, not yet," my grandmother said, putting a gentle hand on his arm. "You'll tell me everything, but we must do it properly." Then she sighed. "Thorbjorn, summon the council."

CHAPTER 22

While Thorbjorn went to wake up the members of the council, my grandmother led the rest of us back towards the village square. We stopped at the garden gate of a house that looked no different from the others around it. We went inside and took off our shoes in the mudroom. It all felt so ordinary.

"Ingrid, stay with Loke," she told me as she headed up a flight of stairs.

"Okay," I agreed. "What's going on?" I whispered to Loke.

"She has to get into her vestments," he told me. He had taken charge of Halldis when Thorbjorn had left and was guiding her up the few steps from the mudroom to the main space of the house.

"Her what now?" I asked.

"You know, like badges of office or whatever," he said.

"But what's her office?" I asked.

"She's the volva," Roarr said. He had been so quiet on the walk here I had thought he had lapsed back into catatonia, and even now his voice was quiet and inflectionless.

"It means she's a wise woman," Loke said. Halldis started to cackle, but we all ignored her. "She has powers, like a witch, but not every witch is a volva. They are much rarer. They have foresight and use it to serve the needs of the community. In this case, us."

"You know nothing," Halldis said to him, and then pinned me down with a fierce gaze. "And you will never be the volva."

Before I could summon up a reply, the room around us was suddenly bathed in light. I had crossed the room in the darkness and had been trying to look out the back window into the night. Now I turned to see that the room was in two sections, one higher than the other, and the edge of the higher section had a modern sort of fire feature built into it. It was like something out of a trendy restaurant, a row of flames that danced all along the edge of the raised floor. Behind the flames, I saw a three-legged stool sitting between two tall, elaborately carved wooden pillars. I couldn't make out the details of the carvings in the flickering flame light.

"Those are your family pillars," Loke whispered to me. "Torfa brought them from the old world."

"Are you saying this is my family's house?" I asked.

"Yeah," he said, and that old grin was back. "Why do you think it looks like nobody lives here?"

My grandmother came down a different flight of stairs. She was wearing a cloak made of feathers. Like the stool and the pillars, it looked old and very fragile, like a fingertip stroking over those feathers would destroy the whole thing. She approached the stool and settled on it gingerly, arranging the cloak around her as she did so. When she had it how she wanted it, she rested her hands on her lap, and I saw she was holding a bronze wand in her hands.

So she really was a witch?

"Ingrid, while we wait, why don't you tell me everything that happened to you since we parted company?"

"Is this official?" I asked. I felt like I was standing in a court of law.

"Official enough," she said. I told her everything and tried not to leave any details out. I was just winding up when we all heard the front door open and then close. A moment later, Thorbjorn came into the room. "They are on their way."

"Very good," my grandmother said. "Thank you, Ingrid. You may take a seat. Now I'd like to hear Thorbjorn's testimony, if you please."

"Of course, volva," he said with a little bow. Loke was waving me over to where he sat on a long padded bench that was built into the wall to my right. I sat down beside him. Roarr was sitting by himself on the far end. Next to Loke, Halldis' breath was a loud rattle that never ceased. With the hair over her face I couldn't tell if she was even still awake.

Thorbjorn set a stool in the middle of the lower part of the room and sat down on it. "Where do you want me to begin?"

My grandmother considered for a moment. "From the moment you left me at the meeting hall."

He nodded, then collected his thoughts. "My brothers and I went out into the hills to patrol. We were looking for Roarr, whom we didn't find. We were also looking for intruders. Those we did find. There was a trio of giants coming down out of the mountains."

"Into our lands?" my grandmother asked.

"I understand that was their intent," Thorbjorn said. "But when we met them, they were not quite so far."

"What happened?" my grandmother asked.

"I think they expected us to fight them straightaway. But we bargained with them. Rather than all of us in a general skirmish, my brother Thorulv wrestled with the largest of them."

"And then?"

Thorbjorn blinked. "Well, Thorulv won. Then we all sat down to drink beer together. That's when they told us that someone had offered them free passage into the new world in exchange for killing the five of us."

"Who?"

"No idea. It was the usual story: shadowy figure in a hood and cloak, voice all gravelly, could be anyone of any age or gender."

"Why did they want passage to the new world?" my grandmother asked. "Will they be back again?"

"I doubt it," he said. "I don't think they wanted anything out of the deal besides a good fight. Which Thorulv gave them. It was a very exciting match. But they took our deal so quickly and so eagerly, I don't think they ever had murderous intent, no matter what the person who had sent them had intended. It's possible the culprit didn't know giants very well. It's very easy to bargain with them when you've brought beer."

"I look forward to hearing Thorulv tell that tale once it's been properly embellished," my grandmother said. "How did you end up at Halldis' house?"

"I saw the light," he said. "It was like a shaft of pure energy that shot up into the sky. I've never seen anything like it, but I knew it was trouble. Especially when I realized where it was coming from. I left my brothers with the giants. Then I ran into Loke standing in the garden outside of Halldis' house, and the two of us attempted to batter the door down. We couldn't do it. I think there was powerful magic on it. But then someone just opened it up from the inside."

"Ingrid, can you explain any of this?"

"Some," I said. "I guess that pillar of light was when Mjolner deflected Halldis' spell. It burst through the roof. I mostly saw the stars, but there was also this purplish-white light that went up forever. Oh, and Mjolner is also the one who broke the spell on the door."

"Yes, that seems to be one of his talents," my grandmother said. Then her face softened as she turned to Roarr. "Roarr, are you ready to speak now?"

He nodded and moved to the center of the floor. He didn't say anything for a long time, and there was no sound in the room but the soft hiss of the gas fires and the rattle of Halldis' breathing.

When he finally started to speak, his voice was so quiet I had to strain to hear. "It started when Lisa left for school four years ago," he said. "She came back to see me as often as she could, but in between times, I was out of sorts. I missed her."

"I told you to find something to fill your time," my grandmother said.

"I tried to. I tried taking some of the patrols, going out into the hills when the Thors were all busy elsewhere. But they generally weren't busy doing anything besides patrolling, so I didn't get a chance to go out much.

"Anyway, one of those times when I was out there, I found something. It looked like a tiny village, but it clearly hadn't been used in some time. And near the firepit, I found that amulet. The one I gave you just now."

"I still have it," my grandmother assured him.

"Yes. So, I found that, but I didn't know what it was. I was going to bring it to you, I swear, but when I came back to Villmark, Halldis was there at the north park. It was like she was just waiting for me. Like she knew what I had."

"It is an artifact of great power. I'm sure she sensed that," my grandmother said. Then more sternly, "but she didn't need that power to get it from you. You gave it to her freely, didn't you?"

"She just had a way of talking," he said, but he wasn't looking up at my grandmother anymore. His gaze was fixed on the floor in front of him.

"She does," my grandmother allowed. "We can come back to that part later. For now, tell me what happened with Lisa."

Roarr pressed the bridge of his nose between his thumb and forefinger, and I could tell he was fighting a losing battle against the tears that were threatening to overwhelm him. When he spoke again, his voice was thick, and he struggled to get the words out. "Yesterday or I guess the day before, Halldis called me to her. It's this thing she does, where I know she wants me, and I can't get her out of my head until I see what she wants. She's been doing that to me since I gave her that amulet.

"Anyway, when I got there, I saw Lisa there, lying on the floor. Halldis was in a panic. She had come home to find Lisa in her house, she said. She said that Lisa had touched something she shouldn't have and poisoned herself. Now Halldis didn't know what to do. She was sure if this girl was found dead in her cabin that she'd be blamed, but it was an accident. A stupid random accident."

"And did you believe her? That it was an accident?" my grandmother asked.

"No," Roarr said, his voice hitching with sobs. "But it was already too late, so what did it matter?"

His sobs echoed through the room, but my grandmother did nothing to fill the silence. She just waited for him to pull himself together and carry on with his story.

"So," he said, sniffling hard as he wiped at his face, "she wanted me to move the body. She was from Runde; she needed to be found dead in Runde. Halldis said to put her at the crossroads up on the highway. I don't know if that's a magic thing, or if she was just hoping that someone would run over her and no one would ever know she had been poisoned. I don't know. But as I carried her down the hill, this fog just lifted up out of nowhere and followed me down to the highway. And it spread out everywhere, so thick. It was like some... thing. Some monstrous thing that would crush me if I didn't do as Halldis asked."

"Ah," Thorbjorn said, then reddened when my grandmother shot him a look of annoyance.

"Then you went back to Halldis," she said when she had turned back to Roarr. "And she did what? Put a spell on you to keep you quiet?"

"I think so," he said. He had his emotions back under control now. "I think that's what happened."

"Are you sure?" my grandmother demanded.

"No," he admitted. "I don't know. Maybe I was always under her spell. Maybe I never was. I don't really know that I can feel the difference."

"Halldis," my grandmother called. Halldis made a low growl but didn't move from the bench or even lift her head. "Halldis, why did you poison Lisa?"

"She poisoned herself," Halldis said in her scratchy crone voice. "She messed in things she should've left alone."

"I don't believe you, Halldis," my grandmother said. "I've known you for too long. I know your house is warded. Those wards are so strong that even a certain cat who can go anywhere he pleases could not get inside until you opened the door."

Halldis just made that growling sound again, but I sensed she was conceding the point.

"Roarr was going to leave," my grandmother went on. "Lisa wanted him to go with her, and his parents, despite all the noise they've made about disapproving, were going to let him. You had worked so hard to harden their hearts over the last four years, but in the end, they valued their son's happiness too much. And all of your plans were going to come to nothing."

"What does it matter? Dead is dead," Halldis said. "Her people are Runde people. I owe them no restitution."

"No, by our laws, you do not," my grandmother grudgingly agreed. "But then you tried to cover up what you did. And you pulled Roarr into your lies. You must answer for that. And for so much else."

Just then, the front door banged open again. Three people came in from the mudroom. The first was a man nearly as large as Thorbjorn, but older. His body was still hard muscle, but his face was lined, and his hair was gray.

The second was a woman of about my grandmother's age. She had silver hair in braids that wrapped around her head, although it looked like she had just gotten up from sleeping on that hair. She had thrown a cloak over what looked like a nightgown, but rings glinted on all of her fingers.

The third was a thin man, also old, leaning heavily on a staff as he walked. He was nearly bald, what hair he had left forming a frizzy halo around his head.

"The council arrives," my grandmother said with a little bow.

The woman frowned then spoke in Norwegian. My grandmother answered in the same language, and then the men were talking too.

"What are they saying?" I asked Loke.

"Right now, they're just fighting over the usual matters of protocol," he said. "You do realize this is why your grandmother started without them? She wanted you to hear the whole story for yourself. They would've insisted in conducting matters in our own language. But don't worry. In the end, your grandmother is going to get exactly what she wants out of them. She always does."

"What *does* she want, though?" I asked.

I don't know if my grandmother heard me, but at that moment, she got to her feet and leaped easily over the row of flames to land on the floor below. Her cloak of feathers spread out behind her, and for a moment I thought she was really about to fly.

But she didn't. She just walked across the room to stand in front of Halldis. Loke and I got up and moved out of the way, but Halldis didn't so much as look up.

"This is the source of all of her unearned power," my grandmother said in English. She held the amulet up for all to see. Then she closed her hand over it, and there was a flash of light. When she opened her hand again, all that remained on her palm were twists of bronze.

The big man said something, and Loke whispered into my ear, "that's not all of her power, he says."

"No," my grandmother agreed. "She is still a danger. She will always be a danger."

The big man spoke again, and Loke told me, "he wants her to be put to death."

"Do you do that here?" I asked.

"Never in my lifetime," Loke said. "But this is pretty rare circumstances."

"No," my grandmother said. "That's not what we're going to do. Banishment will not suit either. She would only become a greater danger on her own in the mountains. No, she will be taken to the deepest cave. I shall seal her in myself. She will remain there for the rest of her days. However many they are."

The council didn't look pleased with this decision, but they didn't argue. To my surprise, neither did Halldis. I wondered what *that* meant. She wasn't the type to give up or admit defeat.

But she was the type to bide her time.

"I'll take her down there myself," Thorbjorn said, grabbing Halldis' arm. Then he gave my grandmother a questioning look.

"Yes, take her," she said. "She's depleted her powers. I will have time enough to bind her to her new home before they return. She relied too long on this trinket." She looked down at the fragments still in her hand.

The councilwoman spoke again, and Loke translated for me. "She wants to know what will happen to Roarr. He also covered up the crime and must be tried."

"I'll leave that matter in your hands," my grandmother said to the council, still in English. "Now I need to put the vestments away and get some sleep. I'm exhausted."

The council closed ranks and whispered together, and I found myself leaning against Loke's shoulder, suddenly quite tired myself.

But Roarr stood alone, shifting his weight from foot to foot and mumbling to himself.

"Roarr," my grandmother said. "You have something else to ask?"

"It's just," he said, swallowing hard, "It's just, it's true what I said before. I don't know when I was under a spell and when I wasn't."

"The council will take that into account. They don't need my guidance on that," she said.

"No, that's not what I mean," he said. Then a look of pure anguish came over his face. "I need to know. Did I do what I did because she had ensorcelled me? Or did I just do it because she told me to? Could I have said no?"

My grandmother took him into her arms and gave him a long hug. But the relief I could see washing over him was short-lived.

"No one can answer that question but you, Roarr," she said sadly. "And I'm not sure if any answer is ever going to satisfy you. You may never know for sure. You'll just have to find an answer that lets you carry on."

She patted his cheek, her face grave, then turned and headed back up the stairs.

CHAPTER 23

I woke up the next morning back in the built-in bed in my grandmother's loft. The minute I opened my eyes, I saw Lake Superior through my little window. And I could smell waffles baking on the waffle iron down in the kitchen.

I swung my legs out of bed and once again recoiled at the cold touch of the wood on the bottoms of my bare feet. I definitely had to get my slippers unpacked.

Wait a minute. How late had I slept? Andrew was going to help me bring the rest of my things down today. Had I missed him?

I dressed in a hurry and ran downstairs, still pulling on my sweatshirt.

"There you are," my grandmother said as I came into the kitchen. "I was just about to get you. Your cat's been keeping me company, but I really wanted to talk to you."

"Do you want me to finish making those? You look worn out," I said.

"No, dear. This is the last of the batter, and then I'll sit down with you. Move your cat off the table; he's trying to get at the butter again."

I picked Mjolner up off the table and set him on the floor. For all of the good it would do. He went wherever he liked.

Which reminded me of a question I had forgotten to ask the night before.

"How did you know Mjolner couldn't get into Halldis' cabin?" I asked.

"That's your first question?" my grandmother asked me as she lifted the lid on the waffle-maker, then pulled out the steaming waffle and added it to the stack on the plate on the table.

"The first of many," I said.

"It was a hunch. Based on what you told me and the timing of things," she said. "But Halldis didn't deny it, so I think we can be pretty confident I'm right. Which, by the way, is the way a lot of this stuff goes. You lead with confidence and rely on being adaptable."

"A lot of what stuff?" I asked around a mouthful of waffle.

"Being a volva," she said. "Do you understand that word?"

"Loke told me," I said.

"Oh, dear," my grandmother said. "More unlearning before you learn."

"I don't know. What he said matched what I saw last night," I said. "I don't think he was wrong with anything he told me."

"Well, maybe not," she allowed. "But either way, you have a lot of learning ahead of you. Studying and practicing both."

"But what if I don't want to be a volva?" I asked. It had been three days since I had put ink on paper, and I couldn't remember the last time I had gone so long without making art. I didn't like the feeling.

"That's exactly what I mean," she said, taking the last waffle out of the maker and then unplugging it. She brought that waffle to the table and sat down beside me. "It's your choice, but before you can make it, you need to understand what it means."

"My choice," I said. "Even though the power descends through the Torfudottirs and we're the last two?"

"Even so," she said. "It's a calling, I suppose you could say, but it's not a destiny. You're not a 'chosen one.' But the role does match your skills."

"I don't know," I said. "I don't think I can do what you do. I certainly can't do what Halldis did."

"More unlearning there," my grandmother said, pursing her lips.

"So the choice is mine, but before I can decide whether or not I want the job, I have to learn how to do it?" I asked.

"I don't think 'have to' is the best way to put it," my grandmother said. "The people of Villmark are your people. They chose to let your mother go out into the world, even though she was a Torfudottir. They welcomed you back as a child, and then let you go again without a fight even though they adored you. Now they're accepting you again, and no one is putting any pressure on you to take on any roles. And they won't, even though they know that I'm getting old and should really have had an apprentice twenty years ago or more."

"No pressure. Sure. Maybe the opposite," I said. "Halldis really wanted the job for herself, didn't she?"

"Yes. And I had been entertaining the thought of training her if you chose not to stay," my grandmother said. "I am sad that Lisa got mixed up in all of this, but I'm very grateful I saw Halldis for what she was before I started her training."

"I thought you always knew what she was?" I asked. I wished I could take those words back; they seemed to cause my grandmother real pain.

"I always knew she was hiding her true face," my grandmother said. "I didn't realize she was dabbling in old magics she didn't understand, or that she was bending Roarr to her will, or playing with the minds of his parents. Or that she was capable of murder."

"Should you have?" I asked as gently as I could.

"Yes, yes, I should've," she said. "Halldis isn't the only one who's older than she looks. I've been working a taxing amount of magic all on my own for decades now. I thought I was managing it all right, but now I know I was lying to myself. Yes, I should've seen so many things that were going on, but I just didn't."

I looked down at the remains of butter and maple syrup on my waffle-less plate. "How long would it take to train me, at least enough to help you?" I asked.

"Not long," she said, but the smile she gave me felt a little forced. She was projecting confidence while preparing to adapt, I was sure.

Then there was a knock on the door. "I think that's Andrew," I said. "He promised to help me bring down the rest of my stuff."

"Yes, of course, go ahead," she said. "You can come find me at the meeting hall when you're through."

"I will," I promised.

It was indeed Andrew waiting on the front porch. But Loke was also there, standing on the grass at the bottom of the steps and looking towards the river.

"Hey, Ingrid," Andrew said with a nervous smile. "I think we agreed to move your stuff together this morning?"

"You don't remember?" I asked.

"We stayed up a bit late last night," he said, "telling Lisa stories. But Jessica was in much better spirits afterward."

"I'm glad about that," I said. I came outside, closing the door behind me before Mjolner could dart out. Then I went down the steps to where Loke was standing. "Good morning, Luke."

"Is it?" he asked.

"You were up all night with Andrew and Jessica and Michelle?" I asked.

"Not all night," he said.

"No, it was at least an hour before dawn when we rolled out," Andrew said with a grin. I raised a quizzical eyebrow at Loke, but he just shrugged. I knew he had been up in Villmark with me since well before midnight. And yet Andrew thought he had been with him all night long? I wouldn't be surprised if Jessica and Michelle thought so too.

We walked together up the path that went under the bridge. I tried to let Andrew go on ahead and keep Loke behind, but it wasn't until we reached the parking lot and Andrew ran to speak to his father that I got my opportunity.

"So is it part of the magic my grandmother does? This thing where you're in two places at once?" I asked. "Can anyone from Villmark do it?"

"No," he said with a wide grin. "And don't tell her. She's stressed out enough already, isn't she?"

"She's a little frustrated with the things you've been telling me. She says I'm going to have to unlearn all of it before she can teach me," I said.

"I've heard that little parable before," he said. "You know, the one where you can't pour knowledge into a cup that's already full. Or is that a proverb? Or an allegory?"

I could tell he was hoping to distract me. "Do you know what she's going to be teaching me, then?" I asked.

"Sure," he said. "You're going to love it."

"Are you being sarcastic?"

"You know, I don't know," he said. His voice sounded strange, and then I realized it was because he was being honest with me.

"You think I really *will* love it?" I asked.

"I don't know what you're going to feel," he said. "Maybe it will be exactly perfect for you. Maybe it will be too confining. So many rules, binding you. Well, you know what that feels like, don't you?"

"I don't mind rules," I said.

"So there's your answer," he said with a shrug.

"I don't know what I'll like until I try it, though. Right?"

Andrew had finished talking with his father and was now walking back towards us, his hands in his pockets and the wind off Lake Superior tossing around the waves of his hair.

"I'm sure you'll figure it all out soon enough," Loke said diplomatically. But then he leaned closer to speak right into my ear. "But if you find that the rules chafe, that like me you long for a different sort of power, one more fluid and with fewer restrictions, if that should be the case, you'll always know where to find me."

I turned to look at him, to try to gauge if he was serious, but he was no longer looking at me. He was smiling at Andrew as he drew up to us.

"Okay," Andrew said, clapping his hands together. "Ready to bring your stuff down and finally call this place home?"

"Yes, I am," I said. But was I?

That would be the other thing I would have to discover about myself. On top of the magic thing and whether or not it suited me.

Was my home in Runde, or in Villmark?

CHECK OUT BOOK TWO!

The Viking Witch will return in Death Under the Bridge, available now!

Ingrid Torfa lives between two worlds. In her life on the shore of Lake Superior she mingles with fishermen and farmers, quiet folk who keep to themselves. But her other life on a hilltop overlooking the lake she lives among the descendants of Vikings.

On top of all that, she trains day and night to master magic, to one day take her grandmother's place maintaining the spells that hide the Viking village from modern eyes.

But life as a witch requires more than casting spells. As resident peacemaker and unofficial impartial judge, her grandmother arbitrates disputes. The residents of both worlds hold her in high regard.

Then a long simmering property dispute between two farming families comes to full boil: a murder. Now Ingrid must find the real culprit before the feuding families decide to mete out their own justice.

Her grandmother needs her. But what if she fails?

Death Under the Bridge, Book 2 in the Viking Witch Mystery Series!

THE WITCHES THREE COZY MYSTERIES

In case you missed it, check out Charm School, the first book in the complete Witches Three Cozy Mystery Series!

Amanda Clarke thinks of herself as perfectly ordinary in every way. Just a small-town girl who serves breakfast all day in a little diner nestled next to the highway, nothing but dairy farms for miles around. She fits in there.

But then an old woman she never met dies, and Amanda was named in her will. Now Amanda packs a bag and heads to the big city, to Miss Zenobia Weekes' Charm School for Exceptional Young Ladies. And it's not in just any neighborhood. No, she finds herself on Summit Avenue in St. Paul, a street lined with gorgeous old houses, the former homes of lumber barons, railroad millionaires, even the writer F. Scott Fitzgerald. Why, Amanda can practically hear the jazz music still playing across the decades.

Scratch that. The music really, literally, still plays in the backyard of the charm school. Because the house stretches across time itself. Without a witch to protect this tear in the fabric of the world, anything can spill over. Like music.

Or like murder.

Charm School, the first book in the complete Witches Three Cozy Mystery Series!

ALSO FROM RATATOSKR PRESS

The Ritchie and Fitz Sci-Fi Murder Mysteries starts with Murder on the Intergalactic Railway.

For Murdina Ritchie, acceptance at the Oymyakon Foreign Service Academy means one last chance at her dream of becoming a diplomat for the Union of Free Worlds. For Shackleton Fitz IV, it represents his last chance not to fail out of military service entirely.

Strange that fate should throw them together now, among the last group of students admitted after the start of the semester. They had once shared the strongest of friendships. But that all ended a long time ago.

But when an insufferable but politically important woman turns up murdered, the two agree to put their differences aside and work together to solve the case.

Because the murderer might strike again. But more importantly, solving a murder would just have to impress the dour colonel who clearly thinks neither of them belong at his academy.

Murder on the Intergalactic Railway, the first book in the Ritchie and Fitz Sci-Fi Murder Mysteries.

FREE EBOOK!

Like exclusive, free content?

If you'd like to receive "The Cat's Hammer," a free prequel short story to the Viking Witch Cozy Mystery series, plus a ton of other free goodies, go to CateMartin.com to subscribe to my monthly newsletter! This eBook is exclusively for newsletter subscribers and will never be sold in stores. Check it out!

ABOUT THE AUTHOR

Cate Martin is a mystery writer who lives in Minneapolis, Minnesota.

ALSO BY CATE MARTIN

The Witches Three Cozy Mystery Series

Charm School

Work Like a Charm

Third Time is a Charm

Old World Charm

Charm his Pants Off

Charm Offensive

The Viking Witch Cozy Mysteries

Body at the Crossroads

Death Under the Bridge

Murder on the Lake

Killing in the Village Commons (coming February 9, 2021)

CPSIA information can be obtained
at www.ICGtesting.com
Printed in the USA
LVHW100928090722
723113LV00019B/591

9 781951 439323